MY LITTLE DISASTERS

DARKEST DESIRES

JORJOR BATTLE

DEDICATION

To my hotties who protect their own

CONTENT WARNINGS

This book is a dark romance. It explores dark themes that can be triggering. Please check over the list of content and triggers, if needed, before reading.

Morally black and gray characters, murder, death, sexual content, self harm and cursing

Playlist

Crazy .... Le Sserafim

Timeless............. The Weekend, Playboi Carti

Hey Mickey (slowed) .... Baby Tate

Never Lose Me .... Flo Mili

Vixen x 9 am in Calabasas .... Ayesha erotica

Oscar Winning Tears .... Raye

Sticky......... Tyler the Creator ft. GloRilla, Sexy Red, Lil Wayne

Mortes Ostium Society

Founded by Jack the Ripper, the Death's Door Society has been shrouded in mystery for centuries. Built as a sanctuary for serial killers to practice their craft, the Society provides care and resources to it's precious members in whatever form they need.

Only the best of the best gather for the Mortes Ostium Masquerade Ball. Once a year, killers from every corner of the world descend on Paris for a weekend to connect, reminisce, and compare their achievements of the year.

Each book in the Darkest Desires series centers around the grand ball, and the love that the members of the society find along the way.

cordially invites you to the

Masquerade Ball

Musée de la Chasse et de la Nature
Paris, France

 | June |

Black Tie

Accommodation Provided

RSVP
Member ☐ ☐ Plus One

Chapter 1

Pandora

Being pretty has never bitten me so hard in the ass before. I've had many advantages to being pretty. To some, paying off my family's debt by fake dating a Mafia henchman is a blessing. Especially since I haven't had to fuck him yet.

But it's not an advantage. It's not even like the Mafia henchman is attractive or protective. No, he's tall and strong, sure, but an ass and controlling. His self esteem is below hell and his insecurities guide every move he makes. I can't stand the fucking man. I like nice men and he is the furthest thing from nice.

Marcel Amos, the Mafia man I'm "dating" to pay off my dad's debt, finally pulls into my damn driveway after the longest date of my life. I hold the sigh I've been dying to let out. The bastard was going thirty-five miles per hour the whole damn ride and taking all the back ways to irritate the hell out of me.

My cheeks burn from the fake smile held during dinner and my high heels are cutting off the circulation of blood to my toes.

Marcel can hardly put the car in park before my door is open. One heel is on the concrete when I hear his weak-ass grunt of dissatisfaction. Rolling my eyes, I glare back at him with a snarl.

His smug, chiseled face turns to me with his finger on his cheek. He wants a kiss, but I want to stab one of my paint brushes through his cheek and watch him bleed.

I drop forward, giving him the fastest peck of all time, and dart out of the damn car. Slamming the door of his sports car, I pull my white fur coat closer over my chest as I make my way to the porch.

He rolls down the window of the passenger seat, not bothering to be a true gentleman by walking me to my door.

"Consider that 1k off your debt," he yells and that makes me turn on my heel and storm back to the damn car. Only 1k? Is he fucking kidding me? It would take forever to pay off my Dad's debt if one measly date was One-fucking-K.

"Two hours of my time is only worth 1k Marcel?" I snarl, leaning in the open window of his car. "Please, you know that was worth five thousand and that kiss wasn't free either."

"Like it knocks that much off your debt." He laughs at me, throwing his head back as my family's enormous debt is thrown in my face. I tell myself the blush on my cheeks is not from embarrassment and instead from the makeup I put on hours ago.

"Learn to count or I'm calling the boss."

"You a snitch?" he growls, but his bite isn't worth a damn cent.

"I'm a bitch too, so make sure you learn to count or I'm calling Daddy and letting him know his men are pussyfooting around.

I wonder what that will do for his reputation," I say before walking to my porch.

My hand hovers over the door handle. I wait to hear his wheels screech as he whips out of my driveway. Taking a deep breath, I turn away from my house and start walking towards my art studio.

Litchfort is a small town outside of Detroit, Michigan that stays away from the crazy shit that a city brings. The town is filled with people who "made it out," including me and my Dad.

Except we didn't make it out. Not really.

The fall air chills my bare legs. My short dress isn't doing anything to keep me warm and neither is my jacket. Pulling out a cigarette, I light it as I walk. Litchfort is one of those towns from aesthetic girly tv shows with little shops lining the streets and sidewalks absolutely everywhere. There are tons of small businesses, and greenery that is sure to have cost the town a pretty penny, but I'd say is well worth it.

It's why I make sure my cigarette butts make it in the trash and not all over the damn garden beds.

We moved here because this was the furthest suburban town we could afford to live in. Except, we couldn't afford it. No, that's where the Mafia comes in.

They offered my Dad a loan with rates illegally high and that was my Dad's only option to get us somewhere safe.

Dad had a real chance of paying off the debt eventually, but now that the new leader of the Mafia took over, our interest rate tripled and, in hand, changed the trajectory of our lives.

I have an art studio about four blocks from my house where I paint... amongst other things. I pay the rent with the profits from paintings and any other cash I make goes to the Mafia.

Not that I make a hell of a lot but, but anything is better than nothing.

Running my tongue over my teeth, a smile grows on my face. I have a prize waiting for me at my studio today. Two prizes, in fact.

One is named Marko Mayfield. He's hanging by his hands from a chain bolted in my ceiling, shirtless and ready for my art.

The second surprise is on his way to my studio. Kohen Harthwarn is my second treat of the night. While he's not on my kill list, he is definitely on my fuck list. He's... well, he's a nice guy packaged into the sexiest man I've ever seen who comes at my beck and call.

Walking up the stairs on the side of the building, I step into my studio. Locking the door behind me, I see Marko Mayfield. His stomach is heaving as if he's out of breath, maybe from screaming his head off for the past hour or so.

He has no idea why he's here, I'm sure. No one ever does. I always set them up to wake up in a serial killer's den. Confused, scared, and exhausted from the hours I leave them hanging for.

"Un-fucking-tie me," Marko demands as I walk in. I stop at his harsh command. The words spit at me as his glare sharpens. Is this how you ask someone to save you? I take in his extremely athletic body. It was nearly too heavy for me to drag here. His sweat glistens over his abs, and for a moment, I appreciate his body. Abs are hot, what can I say? Though, in my appreciation, I noticed the subtle shake of his weakening body.

His glare stays strong on little old me. The viciousness of his eyes lands on me and I'm not too cocky to admit this reaction surprises me. He doesn't know why I'm here. Maybe he doesn't care.

That's... interesting.

He will, in a minute, but right now he thinks he's in control. The fact he's glaring at me instead of begging is one sign and another is his eyebrow. It doesn't waiver, it's completely normal. No scrunch, no raise, nothing. He's not scared. Besides the slight tremble in his body, which could be due to body exhaustion instead of fear, I'd have no indication he was fearful. His belief in himself is astonishing.

"Why would I do that when I spent so much time getting you here?" I ask, sliding my jacket off. I'm left in a short black dress with the prettiest flouncy skirt. It makes me wanna twirl with glee.

Seeing a girl in a short dress leads my victims to believe women get dressed with them in mind, a man in mind, and this would be the only time they'd be right.

Only they're not the right man. My short dress attire is for Kohen.

This line of thinking, that women dress cute for men, is exactly why they end up stuck here with me.

I've had targets think this is a kink exploration or something. As if there was no other possibility for a girl to have them hanging from her ceiling. All that ego dies when they realize this is actually their deathbed. Death site? Death… studio?

"Fuck that, let me down and I won't hurt you," he spits, and I scrunch my eyebrows. Hurt me? I take a hit of my cigarette and cover my laugh with a cough.

"You don't look like you're in the position to be hurling threats, Mr. Mayfield," I say, picking up a clean pallet and a paintbrush.

"When I get down—"

"Does the name May Harley ring any bells for you?" I ask, cutting Marko's lame ass rant off. The name definitely rings a bell for him. I made sure of it.

I'm an art student by day and a serial killer by night. A death angel taking out students at Litchfort University for seemingly no reason.

No one has connected the sexual assaults these men have committed as a motive for their murders. The reports, if there is a report, have been buried under dirty money and favors.

That's fine. There are other, more effective, ways to deal with these kinds of people.

I committed my first kill about a year and a half ago. A football player got handsy with me. He didn't get any further than his body over mine, but the instinct to kill him took over all my senses.

I said no. I said no multiple times. I screamed. I even cried and he wouldn't stop.

So I killed him with a trophy that was sitting on the nightstand. Bashing him over the head until blood covered my vision.

His blood was everywhere. Red painted my pretty dress, my face, everything from the waist up. It was a mess.

I didn't mean to kill him. I was only saving myself, but no one would have cared.

I killed a man, and I got away with it. Well, with Kohen's help. He's such a nice guy. He saw me struggling with the dead body as I tried to throw it out the window of a frat house. He was walking by and saw me. My prince charming.

See, being pretty helped me out there too. What are the chances a stranger would help me out if I was ugly? Probably slim.

I'll admit I thought I was busted. Panic coursed through my body like the blood in my veins. I kind of liked it. That rush.

Kohen didn't snitch. He's not like that.

He's actually like me.

Something about his eyes when they met mine told me he knew the rush I just experienced.

Ever since, I've craved the rush of killing. So I did it again. And again. And again.

Not long after, the Society contacted me about admission into their cool little club of people similar to me. Kohen works for this Society. Maybe he put a good word in for me, I don't know. I joined and now, a year later, I'm a more skilled serial killer with connections all over the world.

Switching my paint supplies to one hand, I remove my cigarette from my mouth, exhaling the smoke, and gaze up at Marko.

He glares down at me with his light blue eyes. Sweat drips down his tanned face, and his jaw is clenched, but he has no fear. Now that I'm here, he thinks he's safe? Is it because I'm a 5'5" girl, he's not scared?

"Who the hell is May?" His voice is rugged, but scratchy.

"Oh, we're playing this game," I say, burning the butt of my cigarette on his chest right above his nipple. His body jerks back as he hisses, but he doesn't get far because of the chain he's hanging from. "Oh, did that hurt?"

I smile as his face twitches in pain. He does his damndest to hide it, but even his best isn't good enough. Shocker.

"No, please, stop, stop, please don't do this to me," I scream like bloody fucking murder in his face. His eyes widen as he stares at me in shock. "Remember May now?"

The color from his face drains resembling a blood bag after a vampire sucks it dry. His jaw can't help but drop the slightest bit and the anger that heated the room before dissipates. He pulls on his chains and now is when he truly realizes the trouble he's in.

I giggle as I toss my cigarette in a nearby trash can. "So you do remember. Good, now we can get started."

May Harley was a student he raped four weeks ago at a fucking frat party.

I was at the same party with Marcel. Of course, that fucking looser wanted to go to a damn frat party. I saw May after Marko hurt her. In the bed. Frozen.

My face twitches as the frozen image of her plays in my head. Anger bubbling up in me at the memory.

I was going to the bathroom and I walked past the room with the door cracked open and May Harley lying there. Frozen, hopeless, scared.

I took her to the hospital and they made a report, but the school made it disappear.

So instead, I followed my natural instinct, and decided I'll make Marko Mayfield disappear. It's only fair.

Picking up some paint from the pallet, I paint his stomach red, the acrylic coming out chunky. It's not my favorite paint but it does the job.

I much prefer dreamy landscapes and oil paints, or even gouache, but for this, acrylic is perfect.

I start with dots. Each touch makes him flinch. He tries to kick at me, but he can't. He's been hanging here for so long his core isn't strong enough to lift his legs up.

Screams, spit, and all the waterworks begin as I paint his skin, but once I'm in the zone, it's too late.

I'm as dead to the world as he will be.

"Who the hell are you?" he yells. This question I do hear. I stop my art on his body and gaze up at him.

"Oh man," I say. His brown hair is wet with sweat and he's crying. His arms must be killing him. Good. I gaze up at him through my lashes and pouting my lips. "I ran out of paint."

"Is this for fucking show? Are you trying to make an example out of me? I swear she wanted it. She's lying. She's a lying whore–"

I let his rambling fall on deaf ears as I break the tip of my wooden paint brush and stab it into the center of his stomach. Blood splatters as he howls in pain. Pulling it back out, I watch as his blood drips on my palette.

This time, his screams are from pain and I smile. I smile so damn hard as he realizes I'm here to hurt him. This smile isn't fake like earlier. The rush of what's coming covers my skin like a blanket and I'm sure my eyes are glittering as I stare at the blood.

I cackle as his eyes widen. "Oh no! I don't think this'll be enough," I say and stab him again, this time ripping upward to create a bigger hole in his stomach.

"Stop! Please stop. Oh my God, stop."

"Did you stop when May begged? Pleaded? Did you?" I ask, digging deeper.

His eyes bleed into mine as I lean close to his face, close enough I feel the urge to try to rip his nasty lips off his fucking face with my teeth.

His nose might be easier.

"No?" I gasp in fake surprise. "Hmm, how unfortunate for you." I lean back to paint the rest of his body with his blood.

Covering every inch of exposed skin, I layer the thick liquid over the acrylic. Moving around his body, I do his back and I feel him go slack in his chains.

Between the bleeding wound and the strain on his body from hanging, he isn't too far from death. Which is perfect because his body is covered in paint and blood and now that the canvas is covered...well. There's not much left to do.

Knock. Knock. The sound has me snapping my head to the door and I nearly skip to the door, my four-inch heels clicking against the floor as I go to open it. Setting my palette and brush on the side table by my door, I straighten out my dress, making sure my boobs perk up against the lace trim along the strapless neckline.

My courier service is here! Which means Kohen is here. Fucking finally. I swing open the door and the moment my eyes meet the wrong brown eyes, I growl.

"Where's Kohen?" I ask the man at my door who is missing his partner. Turning on my heel, I stomp away from the door. The Society has a rule when it comes to their courier service, which is that any Courier must be accompanied by a Guard to ensure no one tries to hurt them.

Kohen always comes with his boyfriend, who happens to be the most annoying fucking Guard ever. Eros grew up with Kohen and they fell in love somewhere down the line.

So my crush has a boyfriend. I never minded sharing.

Eros Warm smirks as he walks into my studio. I let my eyes drop down his body. I'm not petty enough to say he's ugly.

Eros Warm is pretty fucking hot with deep tan skin and brown, molten eyes. That sharp jaw, lean waist, and strong broad shoulders. I swallow the drool in my mouth as he turns to face me. I'd let myself have a crush on him too, but the man fucking hates me.

Maybe because I call on the Society a lot? Maybe because he knows I'm trying to get with his boyfriend? I shrug. Who the hell knows?

"You know he's not dead yet, right?" Eros's voice comes out rugged and like sex on a damn beach, but I scowl.

"You think I'm fucking stupid or something?" I say, taking a dagger from one of my drawers around the room. I quickly jab it in Marko's neck, all the way to the hilt, properly killing him. "Now, where are my slides?"

The Society tracks our kills with blood sides. We don't have to log all our kills, but once we get to eight, we get an invitation to the annual ball in June. I didn't make the cut last year since I didn't get enough kills before June, but this year, I'm making sure I get my kills in.

Marko will be my seventh kill this year, and it's only August.

"Ring?" Eros asks and I sigh, pulling the gold ring with a skull on it off my finger so he can scan it. Each member gets a ring and this holds all our information, and the Couriers, as well as the Guards, use them to identify us.

He does the scanning thing and puts the blood slides on one of my desks. He cracks his neck as he leans on one of my tables, getting entirely too comfortable in my space.

"You can leave now." Taking a blood slide, I open it up and get a drop of blood, not mixed with paint, and close it before handing it back to Eros.

"I could, but we have to talk." He uses my momentary lapse in awareness to draw me closer to him by bringing the slide closer to him. I look up at him, confused.

"About what?" I spat.

"The Mafia," He says, and I roll my eyes.

"It's handled. They won't find out about The Society." The Society must be kept absolutely secret. It's been a secret for over a century and no one knows more than they are allowed to know about them, even the members. Its official name is Mortes Ostium, Death's Door in Latin, but I refer to them as the Society. Their whole goal is to connect serial killers together and give them a space to be, well, ourselves.

"That's not what I'm worried about and you fucking know it." I scoff, clenching my jaw as I look away from his sharp brown eyes. He must not like that since he yanks my jaw forward to stare straight at him.

I know what he's talking about now. He's talking about my "special assignment" from the Mafia. The one thing they asked me to do and if I accomplish it, they'll erase my debt and keep my Dad safe.

The whole reason I don't attempt to kill the whole damn Mafia is because of my Dad. If I can't kill them all fast enough, or all of them together, and they could try to get my dad and I can't afford that kind of risk.

So I do what they say. I play the part of a Mafia girlfriend until the debt is paid off and we're free.

That is, at least, until they spotted Kohen dropping me off at university one day after a kill in the studio. I was being fucking stupid. I called him because without a ride I'd be late to class since my kill session ran over time. I was lying about running late. Obviously, I only wanted to see him. But that little lie got my Kohen on the Mafia's raider. They somehow spotted his smarts from a mile away and decided they wanted him to work for them.

"They won't touch him," I say, and I mean it. I'd rather pay off this debt by acting as a girlfriend and keep Kohen away from it all.

Kohen isn't pure by any means, he works for the Society. You'd have to be some kind of crazy to do that, but Kohen isn't like anyone I've ever met. He smiles at me. Truly smiles at me. He knows about my void, my killer tendencies, and he still smiles at me.

He's warm, and kind, and that fucking smile, God. That smile. He listens when I ramble on about my art, even when he is supposed to leave to cater to some other serial killer. He stays. He understands. He's special.

He has to be mine. It may be selfish, but I love the way he makes me feel. He's the kind of guy you want to dress cute for. Not because you have to, but because he makes you feel so special when he stares at you.

No one has made me feel that way before. It's more important to me to keep someone like that safe. I'd do anything to keep him safe.

"Then it looks like we're on the same page, Princess," Eros says and backs away from the bubble we're in. I let go of the slide. I swallow as I watch Eros leave my studio.

Between me and his Guard, no one will get their hands on Kohen.

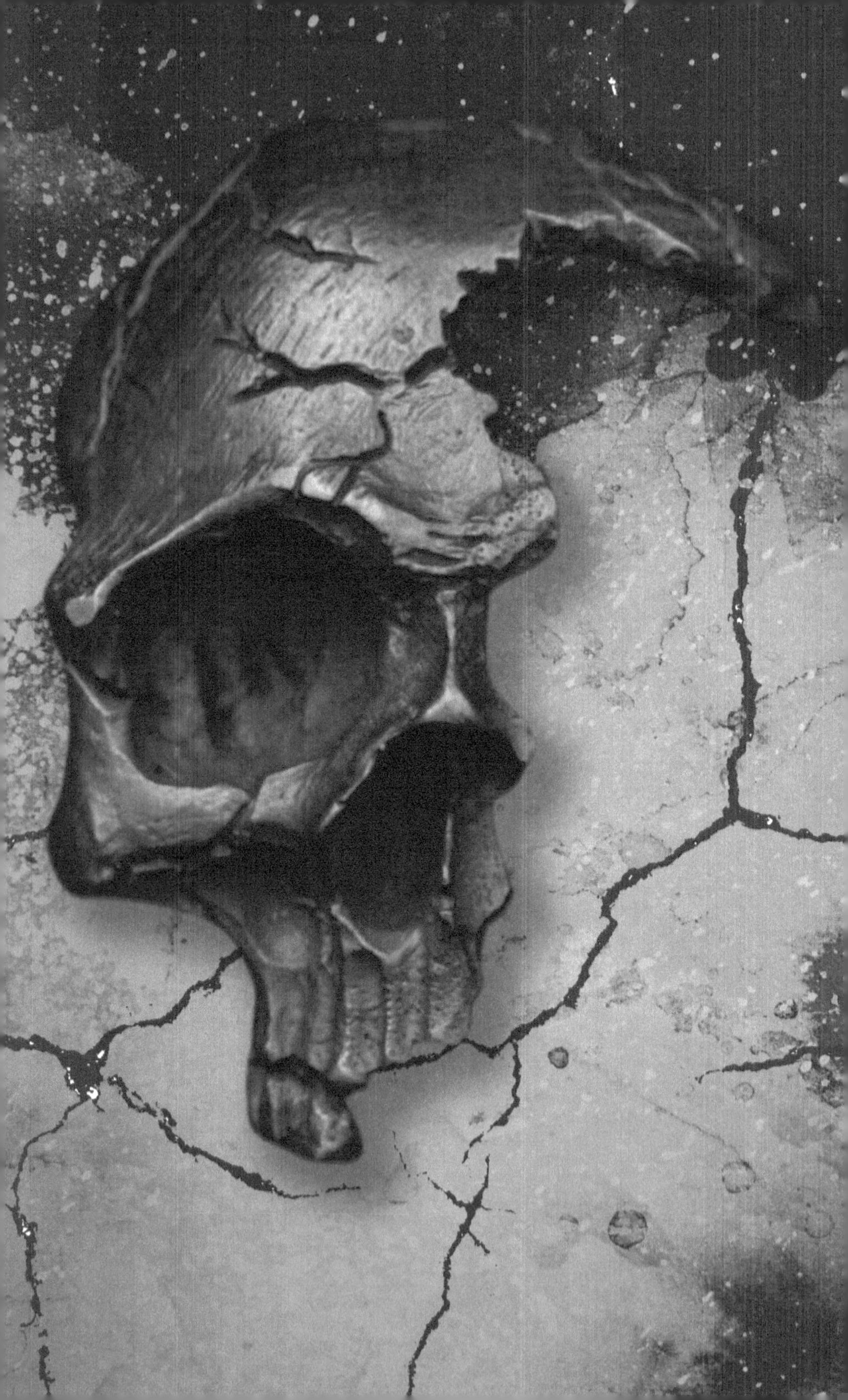

Chapter 2

Kohen

Huffing, I sit back at my desk after completing a delivery of body bags. That crime scene was horrid and I thank God that I didn't have to clean that mess up.

Checking my queue on the computer for the Society, I'm glad to find it empty for the first time today. My eyes drift to my laptop sitting on the desk with the long list of assignments I still needed to do for school. Damn. A heavy weight of dread settles in my chest.

I don't know what convinced me to be a Courier for the biggest secret society in the world and a college student, but I'm paying the price for that decision.

Well, actually, I do know what convinced me. A woman with soft black hair, freckles that danced across her cheeks, and an addicting smile I've become obsessed with over the last year.

I shouldn't have given in to the urge that is Pandora Maci Melrose. But here I am, giving into every urge she draws from me.

She's a member of the serial killer Society I work for. If there was an award for the neediest member, she'd probably win it, though I don't know if she calls on us so much because of the "supplies" she needs or for the company.

Either way, I'm not complaining. I just can't get too excited, thinking she wants to see me.

I am only a delivery boy for serial killers. Anytime anyone needs anything, I am the guy to bring it to them. That's all my job is supposed to entail, yet I went and complicated it by falling for one of the members.

It's not against any rules, so to say, but strongly recommended not to do, by my higher ups.

Eros was conveniently in the bathroom the last time I got called and, as I scroll over assignments, it looks like that asshole took Pandora's nightly call and went without me.

Is he kidding me? I scoff as I scoot my chair closer to my desk to make sure I'm seeing the damn screen right.

He knows her requests are mine. Did he even go with a courier? Who the hell did he go with? I scroll on the request screen and see he went by himself. Why would he go by himself? Can he even do that?

"You mad, baby?" He whispers into my ear, leaning over me. He pecks my cheek and I turn in my chair to face him as he tries to smile innocently.

"You know we do Pandora's together."

"It was fast tonight. She needed slides, no big deal," Eros says, trying to blow it off, which angers me even more. Yeah, it's no big deal, cause he doesn't care to see her. I do. I wanted to see her tonight. I look forward to seeing her every night. I want to see her, stand in her art studio or be on the receiving end of her smile. A sick, twisted run of guilt runs through me at the thought. I want all that and I want Eros, the one man I love, to be beside me. To want me too. I want it all and it's... it's not normal. "You know she'll call again, right? Hell, she might even call again tonight."

"What would she possibly need?" I ask, trying to bury the hope in my voice.

"The moment she thinks of something, we'll be in the car on our way to her," He says plopping into the chair next to me.

I clench my jaw, turning back to my books. I'm not supposed to care for her, yet I do and my boyfriend knows it. Maybe that's why he went without me.

He knows I like her.

I shouldn't. But I can't stop. I tried.

I wasn't raised to have feelings, that's why The Society recruited me. I was always emotionless. I don't feel. Not until I meet Eros. The one man that could get me to smile, even if it was only a little. He got my chest to warm and my cheeks to turn red. I wanted his attention, his affection. I wanted all of him and I still do.

My growing attraction to Pandora is so similar to when I met Eros back in the Society training days. It's confusing. Can someone feel this, this obsession for more than one person?

I am not supposed to. That's what all the relationship books say. That's what social media says, hell I don't even know one person, out of all the people I've met working this job, who has more than one lover. Yet I can't stop.

I want them both. But I shouldn't.

I saw her in the window of some frat house hoisting a dead body out the window, and I was ensnared.

I was hers before she joined the Society and I became her delivery boy.

"Can I say something without you getting pouty?," Eros suddenly says and dread drops in my stomach. I turn to face him. I watch his beautiful face remain stoic, not giving me a hint as to what he has to say.

"We work for serial killers, Eros. I never pout," I say, trying to make sure my lips stay in a straight line. It's not my fault my lips are more round than his. It only looks like I'm pouting, but I'm not.

"Okay, but in all seriousness, Ko, I think you should stay away from her." His words shoot arrows straight to my chest, and I exhale, trying to relieve the pain.

The one time my brain registers emotion is with the two most complicated people on this earth. He knows I can't let her go yet, asks anyway.

"Eros," I say, shaking my head. "Someone has to deliver to her."

"Let someone else take it."

"No." The words fall from my lips before I can stop them. I watch as he throws his head back in frustration. His shiny brown hair shakes as his head moves. Closing his eyes, he runs a hand over his face.

"She's bad news, Ko."

"You just don't like her."

"It's more than that. She's tangled in some shit we don't have to be tangled in." The dread in my stomach switches to worry as I shoot forward in my seat.

"What? What's wrong? Is she in trouble?" I ask.

"She can handle herself–"

"No. Tell me." I try to argue, but he shakes his head.

"It's not our business. She's a member. You're a Courier, I'm a Guard. That's it."

I stop at that, knowing he won't spill if he doesn't want to. I turn back to my books, dropping the conversation. Eros sighs, but I don't turn towards him.

"We said no pouting."

"I'm not," I snap, turning a page I didn't even read. He's right. We're not supposed to get close to members. Not like I have with Pandora.

She's not the first woman to give me attention, but she's the only one I actually want attention from. She lights a fire under my skin and the woman makes me blush. She makes me blush.

I've never blushed as much as I do with Pandora. She's light, airy, and funny yet deadly. She's like me. She can kill people without a second thought, and she's okay with that. She's accepted herself fully as she is, who wouldn't be captivated by that.

I knew I couldn't have her. I stayed back and watched from a distance. Giving myself the small pleasures of being in her company, even if she didn't know I was there. But then things changed. She became a member.

I took over all her deliveries. I enrolled in the same college just to see her. The minute I realized the Society had initiated her, I couldn't stay away anymore.

"We'll do one last 'goodbye' drop, then we do whatever comes in the queue. No more focusing on one member," Eros says, but I let his words flow through one ear and out the other as I nod in fake agreement.

I don't think this obsession can be stopped. In fact, I think it's already too late for me.

Chapter 3

Pandora

Sliding my silk wrap off my head, I get ready for the first day of classes. Enrolling at the local university was Marcel's idea. Since it was his idea, the cost of it comes out of his paychecks. The least he could do for practically forcing me to go was to pay for it.

I know it's because he has a young girl fetish and my 20-year-old ass is getting "old". Going to college was never on my radar, but if he's paying for it, then I guess it would be wasteful not to go.

He can afford it, clearly. I'm a second year painting major at Litchfort University and the tuition for one year is the same amount as half my debt to the Mafia. Not including the interest I've accrued, of course, but still. It's a lot of fucking money.

"Skincare, makeup, and hair," I mutter my to-do list out loud as I stare at myself in the bathroom mirror. I brush my soft black hair and flat iron my bangs so that they are swept to the side.

Walking out of the bathroom, I finish getting ready by dressing in a black miniskirt and a fitted red cardigan before I float down the stairs to see my Dad in the kitchen.

I'm sure he can hear the heel of my knee-high boots clack against the vinyl flooring and yet he doesn't even so much as look at me when I enter the room. I stare at him as he sits at the little kitchen table hidden behind his coffee and a newspaper dated from three days ago. My Dad is a hurt man with teddy bear brown skin and a frown becoming more and more permanent as this 800k debt with the Mafia looms over us.

He's got narrow brown eyes and freckles over his nose, similar to mine. I resemble him so much I don't see my mother's features in me. But, Dad says I have her personality, so at least I have that of my mom.

Too bad I don't remember her.

Clearing my throat, I flip my hair over my shoulder and put on my best smile. My face hurts as if the weight of the fake smile is too heavy for my face and for once, I wish I'd drop it. But I won't. Not in front of the man who risked everything to keep me safe.

"Hey Dad," I say, pouring the already boiled water into a tumbler.

"Hi, honey," He murmurs, still not looking at me. I sit across from him with my tea between my hands, letting the steam warm my face as I brace for another practically one sided conversation with the one man I truly do anything for.

"I start school again today," I say. I'm attempting to get him to smile. He always wanted better for me. It's how we got into this mess in the first place.

"That's great honey. I hope you love it." His smile is tense, but it's better than nothing. I know my dad doesn't hate me. In fact, he loves me. He did everything he could to save me, to save our family, and I'll always owe him for that.

It's why I jumped in when the Mafia made themselves known.

My Mom died in a store shooting when I was a baby. She was collateral, the target being another Mafia member. I was in the cart.

I remember her like a picture, the wide eyes, the fear that bled through the air. I could feel it on my skin and in my hair. Like a curtain being placed over me. The bullet didn't go all the way through, but I picture her frozen, but like she was headed for the ground. That's all I remember.

When she died, my Dad got us the hell out of the city. It's safer here in Litchfort. The only problem with somewhere being safer is that it is also more expensive and, unfortunately, he couldn't afford to move us without some help.

And that's when the Mafia, so graciously, internal eye roll, stepped in.

Now, we have a debt to pay. One that we don't have the money to pay off. So I made them a deal. I'd give myself to them. My time, my body, anything, to help pay off the debt.

Since I've been acting as girlfriend to Marcel, my Dad can barely look at me. I know it's a pride thing, him being a man and my Dad, but, but I'm doing this for me. I need him safe and alive more than my pride, more than his.

"I know I will. I'm going for painting too. That'll waste Marcel's money for sure," I say, though judging by his wince, I shouldn't have. I cringe at my lame ass attempt at being funny.

"You're doing something you love honey, I'm—" He cuts himself off and shakes his head. I know it's not me. I know it's the shame he carries, and yet my soul still cracks at the fact we can't talk anymore. We used to talk all the time. We'd sit at this table and talk for hours. Smiling, laughing, having a great time and now he can't even look at me.

"I'll love it," I say, getting up and pressing a kiss to his forehead before leaving for my first class.

The faster I pay off this debt, the faster we can get our relationship back to normal.

One thing I'm learning about college is that you have to take a bunch of classes unrelated to your major to graduate.

While this wouldn't be the biggest deal since I don't foot the bill for these classes, that also means that when my advisor told me I needed a math credit... I would actually have to take a math course if I plan on graduating, which I do. The least I could get is a degree from all this nonsense.

This semester I'm in a cooking class which somehow counts as a math credit. I didn't ask about the specifics. All I knew when I signed up was that there was no way I was taking algebra if I didn't have to.

Walking into the class, it looks like a standard home ect class with mini kitchens and stools instead of chairs. I hope my skirt is long enough to cover my ass when I sit.

I probably should've thought of that earlier.

I see most of the class must be here based on all the chairs being taken. My eyes scan the room for an open, empty stool but then I see a bleach blond curly head and my heart pounds in my chest.

Is that Kohen? My dreamy, hot, sexy, Society Courier crush Kohen, is in this class? But, he's a business major. What is he doing in a cooking class?

My feet instantly take me to the third open seat at their table. Each table has a small kitchen attached to it, and the table is more like an island with three stools around it.

"Hello boys," I say, sliding onto the stool between them. Of course, wherever Kohen is, so is his dumb boyfriend Eros.

My skirt barely saves my ass from making contact with the publicly used stool and I make a mental note that I have to remember to wear pants on Tuesdays.

Kohen and Eros stare at me as I adjust my skirt and take off my backpack. Eros is more so glaring, while Kohen has that warm smile on his lips that makes them so damn kissable.

"Pandora, I didn't know you were in this class?" Kohen says with a sparkle in his eye. Eros scoffs and it gives the hint that they did, in fact, know I was in this class. Did the Society put them up to this?

"Yeah, God forbid I take math," I say.

"Even though you clearly need to?" Eros says and makes my head snap to him. I glare at his molten brown eyes and his cocky fucking smirk as he chuckles.

"What makes you say that, brainless footman?"

"Well, you requested more slides last night, even though you only needed one more, not three."

"What if I wanted to log four more hits, dumbass?" I snap. How dare he try to call me stupid? He's the stupid one.

"Like you'd do more than the requirement. We've seen your grades, Princess."

"If I wanted advice from a dodo bird, I would've asked you, but I don't," I snap, glaring at Eros.

"Hello Class, I'm Professor Kane. I hope you guys are excited to learn how to cook this semester." The professor drones on as my eyes meet Kohen's side profile. The man is made of every girl's dreams. He's got a sharp jaw and round kissable lips. His skin is lighter than mine, a warmer brown coloring, if I had to get specific. Which I do, regarding my Kohen.

His gray-brown eyes shine against the light in his bleach blond hair. His natural hair coloring is light brown based on the coloring of his eyebrows, but I love the blond.

My daydreaming is rudely interrupted by a swift kick to my leg, and I snap toward the brat in question.

"Stop," I growl.

"Remember what we discussed," Eros mutters as he pulls my stool closer to his by hooking his foot under a bar on mine.

His cologne fills the air around me as his eyes peer into mine for the second time in the last twenty- four hours. I smell cinnamon, and for a moment I'm jealous of how men's cologne stays so strong. His loose t-shirt billows as he leans over me, and I have half the nerve to grip his soft shirt in my hands and yank him closer.

"What part of I have this under control is too confusing for your tiny brain to comprehend?" I snarl.

"Yeah, what was it you discussed last night? Please, enlighten me," Kohen whispers, turning to face us. I go silent as his eyes move between the two of us. Eros doesn't say anything, which confirms that he didn't tell Kohen about my issues with the Mafia.

At least his brain works some of the time.

"Nothing." Eros shrugs, but Kohen's already shaking his head as he hooks his foot under my stool and suddenly I'm pulled closer to him.

This time my frown drops and I'm lost on how to proceed. Kohen leans over me, his eyes light with... with I don't know. The coloring of his eyes darken yet, at the same time, they light as if a light bulb has been turned on behind them. His hand comes down on the island we are sitting at, trapping me in, as his other hand leans against the edge of my stool incredibly close to my ass.

"Tell me Pandora. Tell me what Big Bad Eros is hiding from me." His voice caresses me, and I nearly spill everything. I stop myself quickly, knowing that if I do, he won't want to see me anymore.

His eyes are normally brown but they look darker. Even the white of his eyes look to have a gray sheen over them as he stares me down. His lips turn into a smirk and I have half the nerve to try to bite his damn smirk, but his closeness throws me into a frenzy.

If I'm entangled with the Mafia, if he thinks I have a boyfriend, he won't let me flirt with him anymore.

I can't live without the joy, the rush of flirting with Kohen Harthwarn. The man who saw me throwing a dead body out the window and decided to help me. The man who stares at me like he truly understands me, sees me. I crave the rush I get from laying my eyes upon this man. I can't jeopardize seeing him again.

"Nothing." My voice is quiet as I shake my head. I feel Eros lean over my shoulder, his breath hits the skin of my neck and, oh my fucking God, is it hot in here?

"See, baby. It's nothing," Eros says and Kohen scoffs.

"Yeah, okay," he says as he backs away from us and sits up straight.

All of our stools are incredibly close now and I'm nervous.

I bite the inside of my cheek as I flip my hair over my shoulder, trying to gain any sort of confidence I can, even if I need to fake it.

"This class includes a semester group project and, for the sake of ease, your partners will be who you've sat next to." My eyes instantly find theirs and, while Eros sighs like a fucking child, Kohen raises both his eyebrows as he chuckles.

"Well partners, I guess this secret won't be kept hidden for too much longer now, huh," Kohen whispers.

Shit.

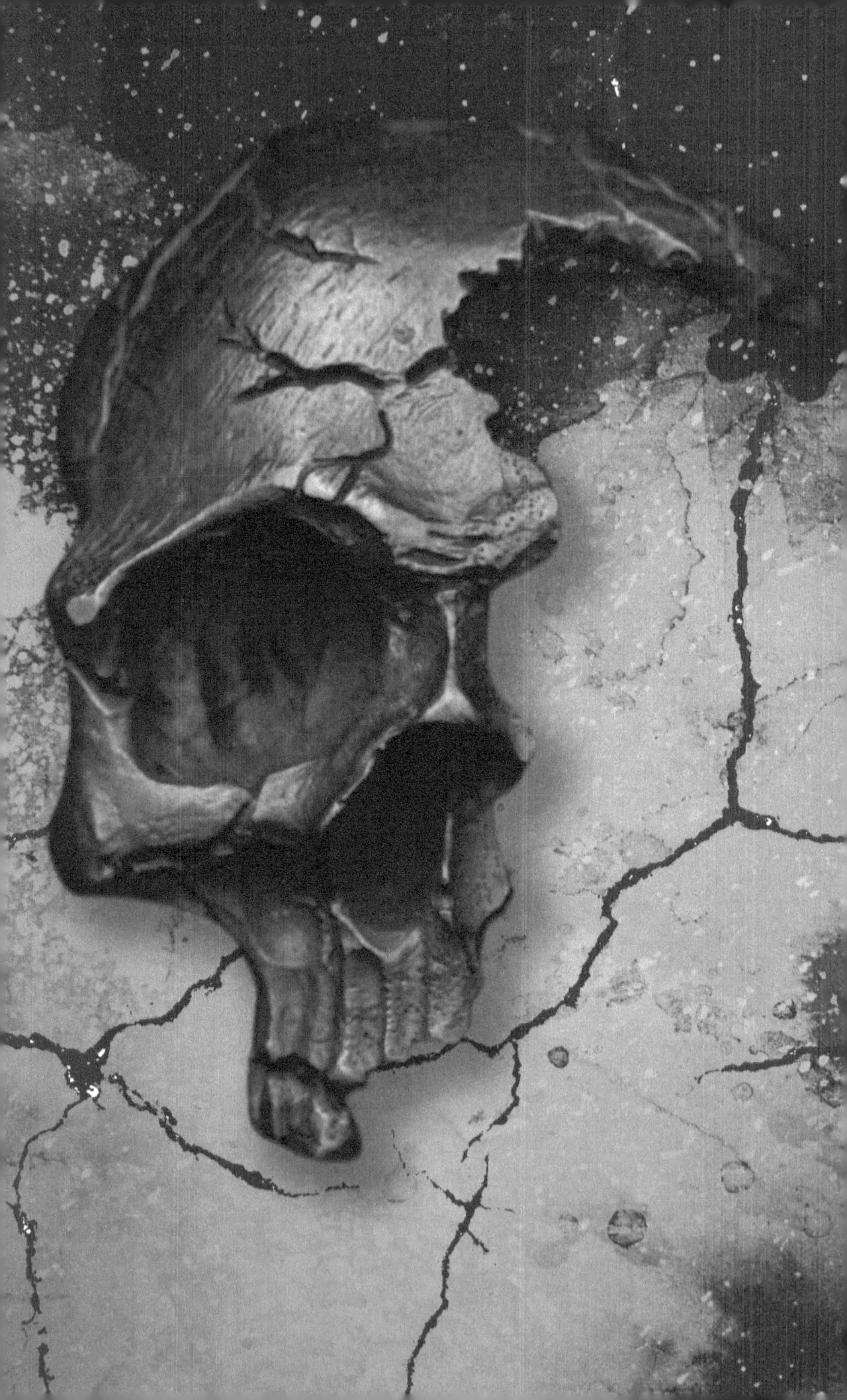

Chapter 4

Eros

That princess just had to sit at our damn table. Now we're stuck for a whole damn semester with her and I don't know how much longer Kohen can hide his feelings for her.

She just couldn't back off like I told her to.

"This is gonna be fun," Kohen says, walking out of the class behind her. She turns and waves her pretty little fingers at us before walking away.

"No, it's not," I snip. Pissed that she's putting Kohen at risk and she fucking knows it. She's wrapped so deep in with the Mafia and she gave them a way in to get to Kohen.

They can't have him. He's mine.

"Watching you two go at it like cats and dogs is always fun," He says as I watch Pandora strut across campus. Stopping outside the brick building, I lean against a wall. I can already tell this is gonna be the longest semester of my damn life.

Keeping these too apart and the Mafia back with a ten-foot pole is surely going to shave ten years off my life. Not that I expect to live very long anyway. As a Guard I could quite literally be killed at any moment. The Society has rules in place to protect us, but since when are serial killers reliable people?

The Society found me when I was 16. After my parents died in a car crash, I was in the foster system for a while. Of course, I had fucking issues, anger issues, fighting issues, all sorts of issues to the point I'd been kicked from so many homes I was on to set a record. I was angry. I was alone. I didn't like that. What seven-year-old likes that?

I ran away. I was fighting on the streets, and that's when the Society swooped me up with the promise of a house, "family", and a stable job.

As a lost teen on the street, a home and a stable job, even with as little information as I knew about the "stable" job, it was impossible to say no. I was cold, hungry, and tired. I'd taken anything.

The stable job they offered was incredibly stable since the only way to leave is to work until you earn their trust or die. As it turns out, they weren't lying about the family bit either. Not only did I meet Kohen, but the folks I trained with as a Guard became my family too. We're close as shit. The things we've done, the dead bodies we cleaned, the fights we've fought bonded us in ways I can't fully comprehend.

"I'm sure you'd like us to go at it in a different way, Ko," I snicker, loving the way his face covers in a deep blush. We haven't talked about our relationship, as in the possibility of adding more people, but I know the conversation is coming up.

On one hand, I'm selfish and want Kohen all to myself, but on the other hand... On the other hand, Pandora, well, no, Pandora is a pain in my ass and that's *it*.

One thing about Ko is that he was never good at hiding his feelings. Kohen isn't used to having them, as in feelings in general. He turned them off before I met him. Now that he has things, people, he cares about he's changing, and only because he's changing for the better is why Pandora is still alive.

Kohen thinks he's hid the fact he has the biggest fucking crush on Pandora from me, but he should've known better.

I know everything there is to know about Kohen Harthwarn like I know how to breathe.

"Tell me what you guys talked about," He asks, stopping beside me and watching the princess walk towards a car. A car I know happens to be owned by Marcel Amos, right-hand man for the Detroit Mafia and Pandora's boyfriend.

"That's the reason we need to stay away from her," I say and kick off the wall and walk in the opposite direction towards my car. Kohen scoffs and follows.

"So she has a boyfriend? So what?"

"So you can't kill him and go on about your merry way," I say.

"I wasn't..." But he was. The Society picked us to work for them for a reason. I was always angry. That was my advantage in this world, but Kohen, Kohen is different.

I may be a fighter, but Kohen is a killer. Kohen doesn't have guilt like I do. He can take a life and not feel an ounce of empathy or guilt. He has those emotions for me. I'd even go as far to say for Pandora too, but when it comes to any other lying thing, its non existence. I look back at my lovely boyfriend who has her pen from class, twiddling between his fingers.

"She's off limits."

"According to who?"

"To me, your boyfriend," I say, though I fucking hate playing that card against him. I turn on the car as he shuts down in the passenger seat and I want to fucking kick myself.

It's not that I don't want to help her, I do, but *we* can't. We can't get involved. Not only does that put the Society at risk, but more importantly, it puts Kohen at risk. We are not heroes. Never have been, never will be.

And now he sits there like a wounded puppy and I need to hurt something besides myself.

I open my mouth, but the words don't come out. I can't rectify this unless I tell him the truth, and I can't. He'll wanna turn into the hero and I can't put him at risk against the whole fucking Mafia.

It's... Its Pandora against the whole fucking mafia.

"Ko–" I try, but I see him shake his head out of the corner of my eye.

"You're right, I'm sorry," He says and my heart fucking crack. God damn this man.

"No, Ko, I'm wrong." I am. I really fucking am.

"No, I'm sorry, I'm in a relationship I shouldn't–I–"

"It's not that. I–I need you safe," I say, turning into the driveway of our house. We don't live far from campus but enough away to drive when the winds are nippy.

"From what?" He asks. We sit in the car for a moment, and I feel our bond growing. I know sooner or later she will be added to our mix and as attractive as she may be, she's annoying as fuck and comes with a lot of baggage. Baggage that we may not be able to handle on our own.

The Mafia is made of at least one hundred men, and each of those men has something to fight for. These men fight to the death, the same as we do, and going up against someone with everything to lose is just as dangerous as going up against someone with nothing.

The new leader of the Detroit mafia is more ruthless than the last. The debt Pandora is trying to pay off will never be satisfied under his rule. If we help her, we'll have to kill all the higher ups of the organization on top of our duties to the Society.

As his Guard and his boyfriend, it's my sole purpose to protect Kohen. Getting involved with Pandora does the exact opposite of that.

"I can't lose you, Ko," I say, shaking my head. I can't. I can't live without him. That's why I became his Guard. I need to know with my own eyes that he is safe.

"I love you too Eros," he says, kissing my cheek before opening the door and getting out. He leans over the car, waiting for me to get out.

"It's the Mafia. She's in trouble with the Mafia."

"The Mafia as a whole or?"

"Might as well be. She's got a debt with them. She'll never be able to pay off." I cave. I can't lie to him, hide from him either. I watch as he processes what I'm saying. Weigh the risks in his mind as he figures out what he wants to do.

"We work for a society literally named Death's Door. I think we can take down the Mafia."

"And get the girl?" I ask, watching as he smiles at me. His face flushes a light red, a reddening you can only see if you look close.

"And get the girl," he confirms.

I scoff as my society phone vibrates. A text for an assignment came through. I see Kohen pull his phone out, too.

"Needs slides, tarp, and–" Kohen murmurs, already sliding on his ski mask for work.

"And bleach. Lots of it." I laugh, pulling out of the University parking lot.

"No. No. Absolutely not. I don't know how many times I can say I have it under control. No." The Princess is not interested in our help whatsoever, a big shocker to apparently only me. Kohen's face drops as she walks back into her art studio.

There isn't a dead body today, but she requested body bags through the courier portal and Kohen was all but on that shit today.

The second we walk through the door, Kohen rushes in, flying toward her as she sits on one of her many stools in front of a blue painted canvas. She was peaceful when we came in. Completely focused on her art, I didn't hear a peep from her blabbering mouth. It was a moment, just a moment, where I believed the three of us could make this work.

Then he went blabbing.

He got too excited and now the Princess was pushing us away. This is admittedly a simple problem with a simple solution.

Don't give her a choice.

"You don't have to have it under control, Pandora, we can help you!" Kohen pleads.

"How did you even find out?" She snaps, glaring at me. I put both my hands up in mock surrender as she turns back to her canvas.

"I told him."

"You told him *my* business, but not *his*?" She raises an eyebrow in challenge and now she's pissing me off.

"Shut up," I growl.

"Oh I'm sorry, I didn't realize you brought your dog here Kohen," she says, staring at me and tilting her annoying little head.

"He wants to help too, despite–" Kohen says, stopping his sentence as if his waving hand over me describes better than words. "Wait my business?"

His head snaps to my direction. His gray-brownish eyes peering into mine with a raised eyebrow.

"Go ahead Princess, since you wanna lay everything out on the table," I say, leaning against the wood table beside her.

Since she wants to open her big fat mouth, she can tell Kohen why the Mafia has their sights on him.

Kohen sighs and peers back at Pandora, who has a sheepish grimace on her face. Yeah, maybe choose your words carefully next time, Princess.

"You're the one spilling beans first, you fucktard," she snips. Sighing, she turns on her stool to face Kohen, who patiently waits for his little Princess to speak.

"Um, well," she says, running a hand through her hair. "The Mafia may, or may not, want you as their right-hand man. In exchange for getting you to join them, they will clear my family's debt."

Kohen doesn't say anything right away. Staring between Pandora and I. His hand is on his chin as he thinks of his next response.

"And you haven't tried to tempt me to join them?" Kohen asks.

"No, you don't belong." At this, I see his shoulders shrink forward before he shakes his head.

"But you'd be free?" he asks and my heart races. No. Absolutely not. He's not considering joining the Mafia right now, is he?

"No." Pandora voices my thoughts before I can speak them. "I'll find another way. You are not joining the Mafia. End of discussion," she snaps. Her loose hair moving with her as she tries to focus back on her painting, but the Princess can't stop staring at Kohen.

"Why don't you want me in the Mafia?" Kohen asks, tilting his head.

"Because you deserve more than those scumbags. The Society is worth your time, not wannabes falling ten feet short. The Society is powerful yet fair and they care for you. The Mafia won't."

"If you'd do so much to protect me, why won't you let me do the same?" He asks and this time I turn the face the Princess. He has a point. Not one I like but can admit is… fair.

She rolls her eyes and crosses her arms. She's given up painting and sits on her metal stool.

"Don't get it confused Kohen, you're mine, and Eros's, to protect." Before she can even get the full sentence out, he's yanking her out of her stool and pushing her so her back is flush against the same table I'm leaning against. Both his hands are around her throat, but not enough to choke her.

She's just as fast with a broken wooden paint brush up against his side.

I scoff at them regardless of the hardness trying to grow in my fucking pants. Shit.

"Harder, Kohen," she mockingly moans though my dick can't tell the difference. Kohen is like a soft teddy bear. With his warm light brown skin and bleach blond curls and round lips, he's a fucking dream. But when he flips his switch. His eyes narrow, and he licks his lips. The damn teddy bear turns into a bloodlust demon waiting for ruby red blood to spill. Especially during sex.

"Stab me Pandora, go ahead, do it." They egg each other on and I'm one skinny thread away from trying to join their pissing contest.

"Let's go, we have another order," I say, trying to leave before this turns into a fuck session we won't be able to stop.

I stand behind Kohen, grabbing him by his neck, jerking him towards me. He brings Pandora up with him and I land a kiss on his neck. I keep my eyes open on Pandora, as her lips widen into a smile I want to wipe off her face.

I want to see her lips part into a round shape as her cheeks flush so deep you almost miss the freckles dancing along her face. Her eyes dark and almost closed as she moans deep from her damn throat—fuck. Stop.

With Ko between us, I look at his hands still wrapped around her slim neck. They are loose now and yet still beautiful. An art piece she won't be able to replicate.

"No one will ever give you what you want. You have to take it, Princess," I say in the space between us before pulling Kohen out the door. The Mafia won't stop. Ever. She will always have them hanging her Dad over her head. We are her one chance to stop them. But she has to take our help.

The ball is in her court. Kohen wanted her permission, so now we have to play the waiting game.

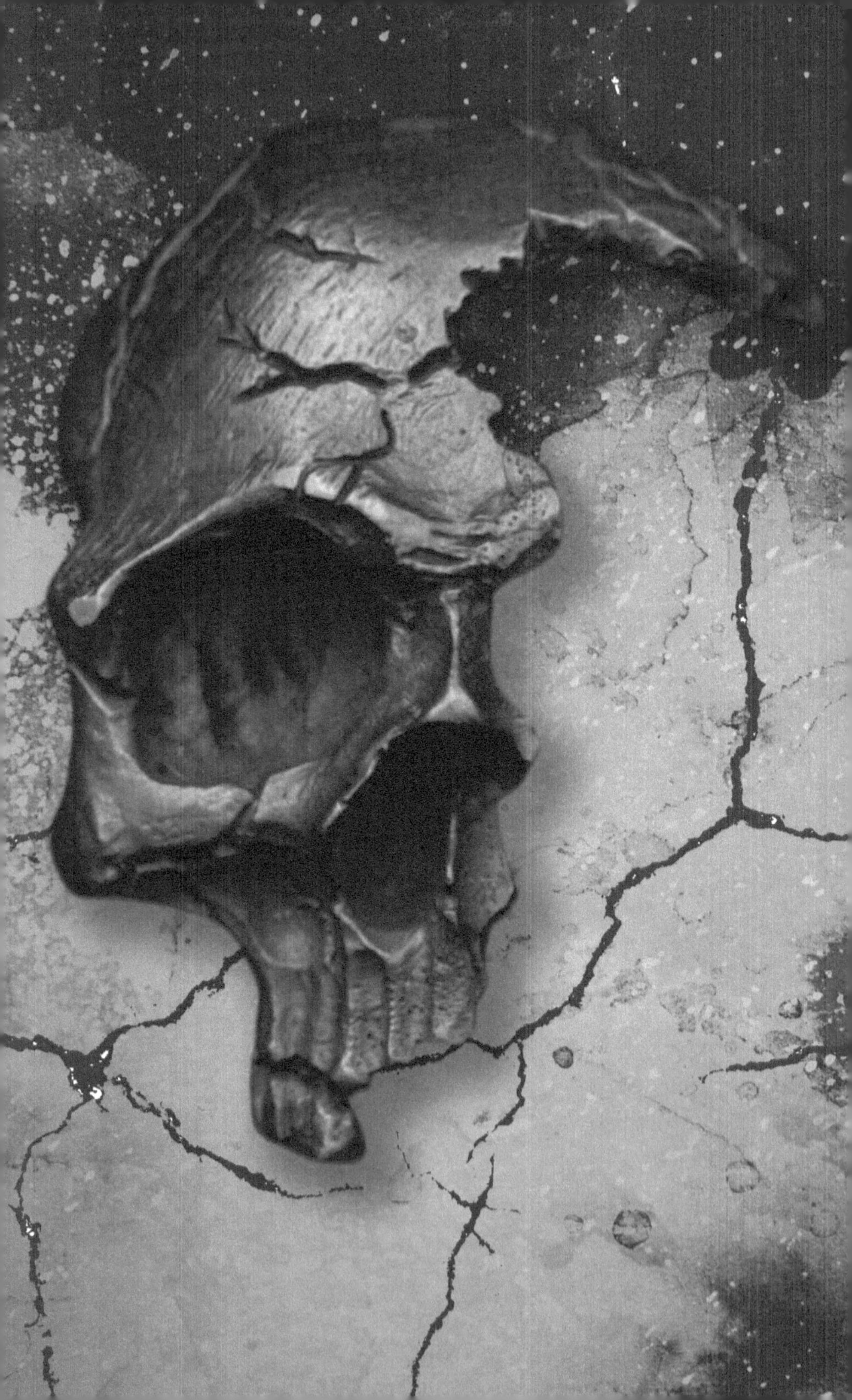

Chapter 5

Pandora

"We saw your girl getting cozy with the target in class," One of Marcel's henchmen snitches as we enter one of the many bars the Mafia owns. I wasn't too far from home and that thought fucking scared me. The Mafia should be in the city, miles away from Litchfort. Not five blocks away.

I fucking hate bars. They are loud, crowded, and stink half the time. That's probably why Marcel likes them. It's a little past noon on a Friday and this bar is packed with day drinkers and smoke.

The bar owner must only be able to see the color purple because nearly everything in here, from the tables, to the booths, to the bar, is varying shades of purple. It's hideous. The disco ball in the upper right-hand corner is on and glittering in all the wrong ways, bleeding light into my eyes every half turn.

"Oh, is that so? Did you bring us up?" Marcel asks, drawing one of his dry ass fingers over my chin.

"Yeah, I was all like 'so this is our first time talking, but do you wanna join the Mafia? They really wanna lick your balls.'" I barely get the sentence out before Marcel shoves me towards the table, squishing my stomach so hard I'm sure there will be bruises.

I take that bruise for the ego shot any day.

"She's in a group project with one of them." The same guy pipes up like he'll get a damn reward or something. When the Mafia Don, Bruno Yearwood, told me he's got his sights on Kohen Harthwarn, I nearly vomited.

A random ass dinner turned out to be not so random when Bruno told me what he wanted. He wanted me to recruit Kohen for a special project he was working on. If I got Kohen to work for him, my family's debt would be cleared. That was three months ago, and I still remember the shock flowing through my body like it was yesterday.

I knew he looked too damn interesting for his own good.

"And how the fuck would you know that?" I snip. The guy is so unimportant looking I wouldn't recognize him from some random ass joe on the street.

"I'm in the same class. You didn't see me?" he asks as if he's truly confused. Honestly, this is the first time I've seen him, or at least remember seeing him.

"Really? Who the hell is paying for that?" I ask, but my question gets left unanswered as the nameless prick glares at me.

"You think Marcel wants you to be left unsupervised on a college campus? We can't have you stepping out on him. That makes us look bad." Another guy I don't know the name of rolls his eyes. Part of the deal is that I remain exclusive to Marcel and the Mafia and of course I made this deal before I met Kohen about a year ago, but... but even then it wouldn't have mattered.

I was put in a dangerous situation with no real way out.

"So what's the plan, Dollface?" Marcel asks while ordering a drink. Fuck, I need one too for this conversation, except Marcel wants me completely sober.

It was unfeminine to drink, he'd say, but I think it's because he likes to exercise the control he has over me. I may run my mouth a lot, but I pick my battles with Marcel and drinking is not one I have the energy to fight him on.

I let out a dramatic sigh as I roll my neck. I didn't dress to be out at a bar. I'm sweating to death underneath my loose gray sweater and black fitted skirt.

I guess I could take off my sweater and walk around the bar in my bra, but I have a feeling Marcel is particularly aggressive and I'm not completely fucking stupid.

I can feel my makeup shift on my face, my foundation running along with the sweat that drips down my face as I scoop my hair up into a bun. I'm glad it's dark as shit in here.

"Well, I have to get to know him first, right Marcel?" I say, giving the dumbass the credit for the obvious plan in the universe.

I'm not talking Kohen into joining this band of freaks. Not a fucking chance. I need more time to figure out how to get my Dad from under their thumbs before they find that out.

Kohen is too perfect to work with the likes of them. He's accepting, he's understanding, he's funny as hell, and most importantly, I like him. I like him a lot. For that reason alone, the Mafia can't have him.

The Society takes care of him and for a society for serial killers, they protect their own with the seriousness of a mama bear. Now that I think about it, I think that mama bear is a really fair comparison for the Society. They protect their cubs so much, so breaking any rules is basically a death sentence in its most horrific sense.

I wish I owed a debt to them instead of the damn Mafia.

"As I instructed," Marcel gloats to his lackeys. My eyes roam to the clock on my phone, gosh how much longer do I have to be here? "Then once he gets in close, she'll find something on him, something he'd risk his life for, and by then we'll have him in the palm of our hands."

I nod like I'm agreeing, but Marcel is forgetting one little detail, two actually.

One, I already know what, well who, Kohen would risk his life for and that's Eros.

Two, that Kohen is his replacement. Marcel is Bruno Yearwood's right-hand man... Bruno is the one that wants Kohen, not Marcel. Meaning Bruno wants him higher in the ranks and by the tension between Bruno and Marcel, Marcel is on his way to Lake Michigan in a body bag.

I've heard them "stern talking", because Marcel would cut off his pinky before he'd yell at Bruno, in secret corners and by the dirty jobs Marcel's been given. I think they are on bad terms.

Could also be a reason Marcel is angry all the fucking time now. You can't trust emotional men who make snap decisions and that is the exact definition of Bruno.

None of us know when the man will snap and kill us. It's slowly breaking down the Mafia hierarchy from the inside out.

The problem is, I could wait my time out until the Mafia dismantles itself, but that sort of distrust takes time I may not have.

I'm not tough enough to hide that Marcel scares me.

"Alright boys, we have work to do," Marcel says, snapping his fingers. The lackeys get up and disappear as I remain seated.

"You come with me." Marcel tries to command me by curling his fingers toward himself, but my duties here are done. I don't leave with them, ever. I wait for everyone to leave, so I know no one follows me.

"Come with you?"

"Isn't that what I said, Dollface?" He sighs and yanks my wrist, dragging me through the incoming crowd of the bar. People bump into me like I'm a fucking fish in a crowded bowl being whipped about. It's fucking pissing me off.

"What the hell do you want, Marcel?" I try to yell over the people, but I think he doesn't hear me, or he doesn't care to answer as we make it outside.

"Fucking unhand me—" I yell, but his hand is gone from my wrist and swinging back towards my face. My head snaps to the side with a sting I'm not used to.

A million thoughts race through my mind. The first one being to jump on Marcel so that I could reach his eyeballs easily enough to dig them out. Then I remember that Marcel is trained in combat, being raised in the Mafia, he's been in more fights than I've killed people and as an opponent I'm not stupid enough to forget that. Plus, the man is six foot and while my victims are tall, they don't know how to throw a real punch like Marcel does.

The biggest realization at this moment is that I'm unarmed. Which is probably a good thing. I should have a gun on me at all times, being a serial killer and all, but even then I wouldn't be able to use it. Not against Marcel. That'd be taking a shot against the whole damn Mafia and that's not a battle I can fight alone.

I grab my cheek as I stumble away from him, but I don't get far. He's yanking me by both arms back to him.

"Don't you ever speak to me like that, I let you get away with far too much Pandora and it's about damn time you learn your fucking place," He roars, hot breath and spit hitting my face making me recoil.

"What the hell are you talking about?"

"This. You running your fucking little mouth with no damn consequences. Well, that shit changes today. It's been a whole year of this shit and I'm sick of it. It's not fucking cute."

"It was never supposed to be cute, dipshit."

"And the next name outta your dirty little mouth better be baby or daddy, or I'll fill that mouth with my fucking cock and see how you like that shit."

"You can't fucking do that. It's part of our deal," I say, knowing the man is dead fucking serious and I'm losing my ammo.

Shit.

He racks my body back and forth in his punishing grip. Even though I'm staring straight at him, I'm back to the day I found him, Bruno, and five other guys in our house.

The day that got me where I am today. Fresh from cleaning up a kill, I waltz into my family home to find three guns pointed at my dad and Bruno asking about the money we owe.

I kill people for sport and yet, walking into this scene, I felt so fucking... fucking powerless. Who the hell am I against three guns and seven men.

I'm nothing.

"You think I care about the deal? You think Bruno does? The deal was only a false pretense you fucking fell for. It's easier when bitches accept their place, but it didn't fucking work. Force is the only way you'll listen." He shoves me back and I fall on my ass like a baby deer. My legs wobble, trying to hold my skirt closed. The skin of my hands breaks against the concrete as I hold back the tears begging to spill over my cheeks.

I didn't want to admit I was living in a bubble. In a bubble of hope that I'd get the relationship with my dad back after this

Mafia mess was handled. That I'd maybe even get the guy and his boyfriend, too. That I would be clean and clear of the Mafia some day.

Except I'm not. I won't ever be, and everyone knew that but me.

"No one will ever give you what you want. You have to take it, Princess."

Fuck. I throw my head back in a lame attempt to keep my tears in check. I hear his spit attack before I feel it. His gob rolls down my fuzzy sweater as I hear Marcel walk away laughing.

Swallowing my pride, I refuse to look at anyone who is trying to enter the bar. I know even if they wanted to help me, they couldn't do shit. Everyone knows Marcel is Mafia and intervening means insulting the Mafia. I know I was on my own for this one. No real gentleman was gonna defend my honor here. Not in this part of town.

Getting off the ground is a harder sucker punch to my ego than being pushed on it. I smooth down my skirt and sweater and fix my bun as I take the walk back to my house. Sniffling in the fall breeze, my lungs and soul cramp with pain. Fuck. How do I fix this?

Eros is right. Of fucking course, the brute was right.

The Mafia was never going to let me go. I was going to be indebted to the Mafia until I got old and ugly and once that happened, they probably would've killed both me and my dad.

I was never going to survive this. No one does.

I feel the blood in my face vanish as my tears dry up. My cheeks feel heavy as the realization of what I have to do showers over me.

I have to kill the Mafia.

And I can't do it alone.

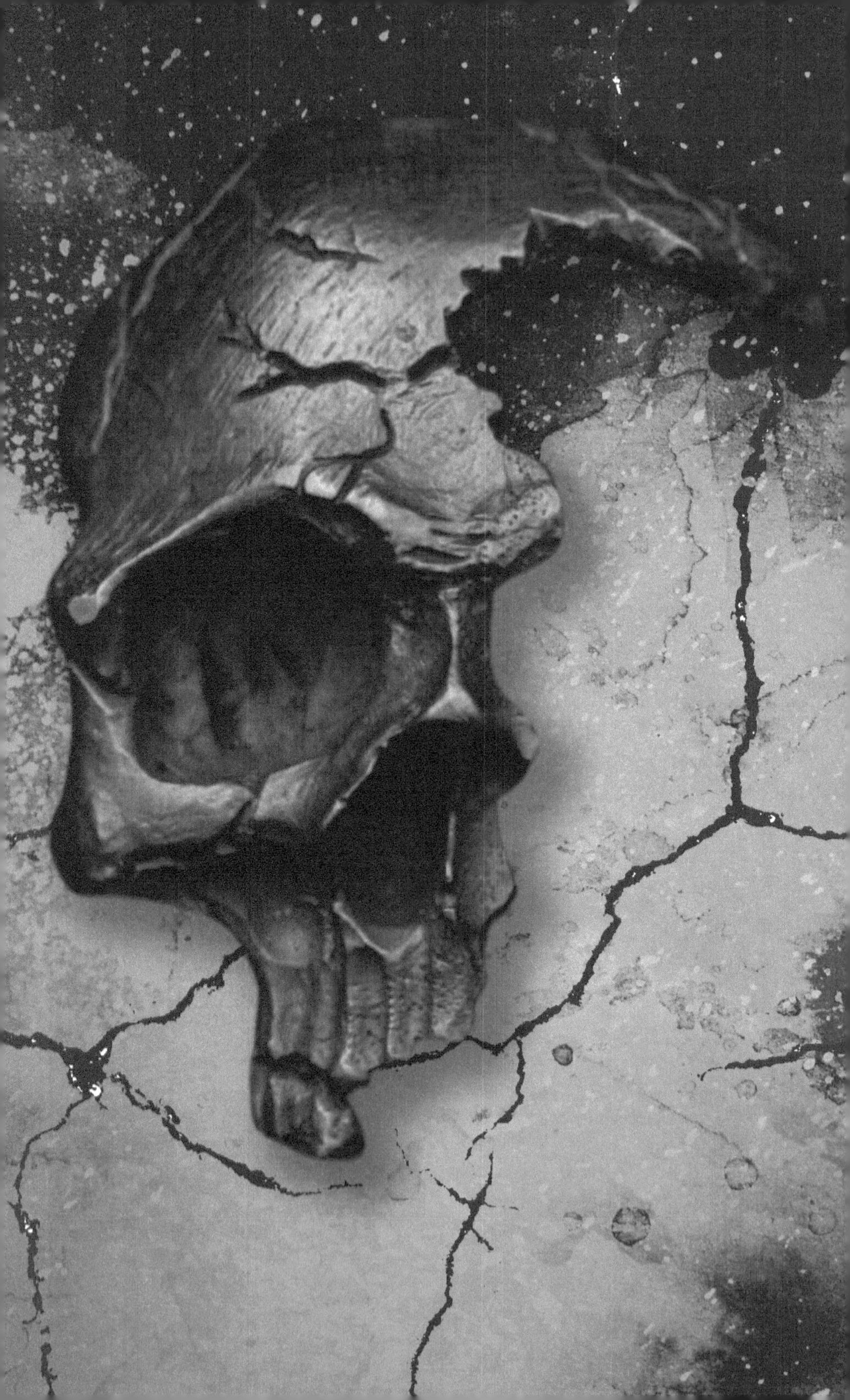

CHAPTER 6

Kohen

"What the fuck?" I hear Eros's voice as he opens the front door of our house. "Who did this? Tell me right fucking now!"

The anger in his voice gets me hopping over the couch and rushing to the front to see what he's talking about. My ratty sweatpants and loose t-shirt completely leaves my mind as I go to see our company at the door.

Turning the corner to the entryway hallway, I see it. The thing that made Eros jump from neutral to pissed in seconds. I see her and my fingers twitch.

I stop in my tracks, unsure of what my instincts will do.

I'm the calm to Eros's storm. That's how it's always been. I was scooped up by the Society when I was 14. I met Eros in the training room, already fighting three other recruits before the class even started. I am his calm and he is my storm.

The chill racing over my face and arms isn't the kind of calm that saves people. That helps Eros knock his anger down from a ten to a two.

This chill isn't one I get often and yet seeing her has made it come on in three seconds.

I want to kill.

My hands instantly reach for Pandora's face. I refrain from touching the big fucking bruise forming on the side of her face.

She stands in a rumpled gray sweater and a dirty skirt and I know this is not right. It doesn't take a year's worth of stalking her to know that something about this picture is wrong. My hand finds her unblemished cheek and she leans into my hand.

My heart pounds in my ears as my eyes meet hers. Her skin is wet from the rain, maybe tears too, and yet soft under my hand. Using her pulse, by the breath that hits my hand on her cheek, I match my breathing to hers. Her breath is calm, collected, and mine is everywhere. It's short, angry and I can't be that right now.

I can't be angry for her. I can't even be angry for myself. I have to be calm. I have to find a solution, a name, to our problem.

Moving my hand from the side of her face, I gently grab her arm guiding her to the kitchen where I sit her up on the counter. My mind's racing, but I know one thing. One entity that's been a problem for her for a while now. One I wished I knew about sooner.

"It was them, wasn't it?" I whisper as Eros comes back with a warm towel. He gently squeezes between us, wiping her face, making sure not to touch her cheek.

The thing about Eros is he's a hard ass with a heart. As much as he tries to play like I'm the only one with a crush on Pandora, I can tell he does, too. I felt his fucking hard on in her art studio.

She doesn't say anything as he cleans her face and neck, then he moves down to her hands and we see the scratches and dried blood drips there too. Her lips are straight and her eyes... her eyes are dull.

She's watching me. I can feel her gaze and yet I'm too damn shy to meet her eyes again. I see Eros's hands over hers and I like that image. The one of them together.

Swallowing my emotions, I turn away to the fridge as my excuse for not meeting her eyes again. I grab an ice pack and wrap it in a kitchen cloth before bringing it to her. She doesn't move to grab it, she merely stares, and that's when I look into her brown eyes again.

"It was." Her voice rasps. I slowly nod, bring the ice pack to her cheek. It was the Mafia. I don't know what changed in the last twenty-four hours, but something has shifted.

The air touches my skin like fog as the rain beats down on the house.

I move my gaze to Eros, who was already staring at me. I swallow my nerves again before looking at Pandora. She attempts to raise her eyebrows before grimacing.

"The boyfriend?" Eros asks, leaning back on the counter opposite of the island. Everything felt like it was going into slow motion.

She nods once, her gaze on the fridge behind me. "You were right."

"Right about what Princess?" Eros says. She pauses. Her eyes flicker to him and I watch as she bites the inside of her cheek.

The smooth brown skin of her cheek creates a dimple as shifts her weight from side to side.

"I need help," she mumbles as a tear slips from her eye. It fucking hurts. It's like a bullet tearing through my own damn cheek, seeing that tear fall from her eye.

"We know," Eros says and guides her to jump off the counter. I know he's taking her to the living room.

I follow close behind them, nerves tickling my arms as she sees what we've been doing.

See, when she said she didn't want our help, I... I didn't listen.

I couldn't. The mafia has her trapped and I couldn't sleep knowing that. I couldn't go on and wait for her to ask for help. This is Pandora Melrose. I didn't think she'd ever come around.

So I gathered information.

I have names of those with the most power and where they live, their families, alive and dead. I have everything down to their favorite restaurant and if they have pets. I couldn't rest.

"Hmm, you are not good at listening, I see," she murmurs. She goes to take a closer look, but Eros stops her.

"Go take a shower Princess, Kohen show her where the bathroom is," He orders. Pandora snickers as I get red in the face.

I don't mind Eros bossing me around. It's... it's different with an audience though. The red covering my face is new and yet the smile it brings to her face settles something in my chest.

"Let's go, Ko." She smirks as she grabs my hand. Her fingers grip mine tightly as I lead her away, walking upstairs to one of the main bathrooms before pausing.

"Oh wait, these don't have soaps yet," I murmur to myself. "You'll have to use my bathroom."

"Even better, can I wear your clothes too?" She chimes. I stand still as I watch the light flood back into her eyes. Her lips curl upward and I let out a breath of relief. My girl is back.

"Yeah, if you want to."

"Oh, I more than want to." I take her to my bathroom inside my room, grabbing towels and a fresh set of clothes for her.

Grabbing the smallest pair of sweats I could find and I turn around to hand them to her.

"Kohen." She smiles and tilts her head, her long hair falling behind her shoulder.

"What?" I ask, confused.

"Can I have some shorts?"

"I have some basketball shorts here somewhere," I say, going back to my dresser.

"Ahh, these'll work." I turn around to face her and she has a pair of my boxers in her hands. The red that was cooling off from earlier is now back tenfold.

"Let's get you into the shower," I say, trying to urge her to the bathroom.

"Aren't you going to join me?" She laughs, throwing her head back and I can help but chuckle too.

"No," I answer. "We have work to do downstairs."

"Booo."

"Meet us downstairs," I say before her hand is gripping my arm and her eyes go from warm to frazzled. They widen and the whites of hers show more as she stares at me.

"No, uh, could you stay here?" She asks, and I freeze. She's panicking...is she afraid to be alone? That can't be it? Can it? Was there something else? Someone else?

Stop. No. Not right now. I nod my head yes and make a show of sitting on my bed with my back to the bathroom door.

The door shuts and I hear the lock click into place as I stare at my room.

My room is pretty plain, but that's how my room has always been. A bed, a dresser, and a TV I've yet to use.

Eros and I recently moved into this house. We lived at the Society's base in Michigan for most of our lives before we graduated from the training system and were able to move out. With the money Eros had been saving, he bought us land and had our dream home built.

Still, I thought I'd finally have a messy room, or at least a room with more personality. At the base, all we had was a bed and a dresser in a room shared with ten other people.

Maybe I'm boring to my core.

Maybe that's why I crave love from more people. I've devoured Eros and now I'm hunting for the next person to consume entirely.

I completely took over Eros's life and it's not enough.

"Stop." My head shots to the open doorway where Eros leans against the frame with his arms crossed. "Don't give me that doe eyed look, Ko, I know."

He can read me like a damn book. I still can't tell if I find it irritating or endearing. I turn away. Embarrassed to be caught spiraling.

"I chose you, and I followed you," He says walking over to me. He stops right beside me. He yanks me by my neck to face him and captures my lips with his. Gnawing at my lips with his teeth and I kiss him back. I love the texture of his lips against mine. The warmth of him choosing me. His lips remind me I'm his as much as he's mine. That this relationship is mutually desired. "And don't you ever fucking forget it."

"And what if I do?" I ask.

"Then I'll just have to remind you."

"So you won't get in the shower with me, but you'll fuck him outside the door and not even invite me, Ko, honey, you break my heart." Pandora's voice snaps me away from Eros as I turn my head to face her.

Big fucking mistake.

Her hair is dry but in a bun with a hair tie she must have kept who knows where, dressed in my t-shirt, which would have covered the boxers she found if she hadn't tucked a bit of it in. She stands with one hand across her stomach and one holding her unbruised cheek.

She's beautiful in my clothes. She's always beautiful. Of course she is. But in my clothes. In my house. In my room. With Eros standing over me and her, watching.

Fuck.

"He's mine to do with as I please Princess, whether you're involved or not," Eros jeers as he kisses me again. I can't help but kiss him back, but I'm much more shy with an audience. What was I thinking? Could I add a third to this party? Could I handle it?

His lips whisk all thoughts away as he presses harder, shoving his tongue past my lips to fight against mine.

The bed is weighed down behind me as delicate hands trace up my arms. She tucks her head in my neck as her arms snake around my abdomen. She yanks me back, my lips snatched away from Eros, who smiles evilly, as I unconsciously lean back into Pandora's embrace.

"You know sharing is caring Eros," she says without moving her head from the crook of my neck. Pecking my neck, her soft lips consume me. I stare at Eros's face as he watches the scene in front of him.

"I don't have to share. He's my boyfriend." He tackles my calves and yanks me back to him. Are they fighting over me right now? Is this real? All I can see is Eros's shirt and for once, I'm thankful for it.

"Well then," she dramatically sighs. The bed moves under me as she crawls off the bed. "I have a Mafia to take down. Let me know when you boys are finished."

I hear her footsteps leave and I lay back flat on the bed. Seeing Eros's face, he's smiling.

"What?" I ask. He's smiling, yet I thought he'd hate fighting with Pandora, even mockingly, as they did. Eros was never a sharer. He doesn't ever share. Not food, not books, or attention. Not until he accepted me into his circle.

"That was fun," He murmurs, kissing my forehead before backing away. "You might wanna fix that before coming down."

I don't need to look down at my pants to know what he's talking about. Sighing, I slide off the bed to take my own cold shower.

Chapter 7

Pandora

Eros gets on my last fucking nerves. Every time I say something, he has to argue like a damn child. Sitting in their living room plotting our revenge is taking up far more time than it probably should. I could've been home hours ago, but it's not like someone is home worrying about me. Dad's working the overnight shift at the grocery store doing inventory. When he finishes that shift, he comes home to sleep for two hours before going to his next shift.

He works as much as he possibly can, his money going back to the Mafia, to get us out of this situation. But he won't last long like this. I need to kill our problem before our problem kills him.

"Why start at the bottom of the food chain? Just hit the head and move on." Eros is pacing behind the couch. He runs his hand through his brown hair every so often, making it more messily sexy.

"Is that all you do? Just hit the head and the job's finished? *Oh poor* Ko—" I say, my own laugh cutting me off. His glare would shut up a sane person, but I can only register the warmth growing in my cheeks.

His glare doesn't stop Kohen's laugh either. The warmth in the room nearly chokes me with happiness I'm not used to.

"You knew what the hell I meant." Okay, maybe *I'm* the one that is arguing. Eros is so easy to rile up, and it doesn't help that he's hot when he's frustrated.

Eros is the only guy to ever talk back to me. Something about that dominance calls to me. It sits like a warm blanket over my skin. He takes the pressure of being the strong one, the leader, the fixer, off my shoulders. There's a strength in him that bleeds through him that is insanely appealing. Addicting to be around.

"We have to take them all out or it won't work," I say. "The new Don will take over my debt, and then I'm in the same predicament as before."

"Before?" Kohen asks. He sits on the couch while I'm seated on the floor closer to the coffee table, with all sorts of documents spread all over it.

"Bruno's only been in charge for a year. Before him, there was Amias Vontelli. Our original debt was with him and though he had high interest rates, we had a chance of paying it off."

"What changed?" Kohen leans forward when I speak. He rests his elbows on his knees and gosh, he smells so fucking good. A mix of fresh water and some good ass laundry detergent.

His shadow covers me as I watch him. His fingers twitch like he is aching to do... something. Take something? I'm not sure, but whatever he wants, he had to know by the point I'd give it to him.

Unless it's not my permission he's waiting for. I glance at Eros's pacing form and I look back at Kohen, whose stare hasn't left me.

"Bruno's even more greedy. He wants more than money. He craves power in all forms. I should've realized that sooner maybe I wouldn't of have to play fucking girlfriend."

That's a lie too. I played right into this fate. If not for playing fake girlfriend, my Dad would be dead. Maybe that's why I didn't fight it. I knew deep down, this was how this would play out. I'd be trapped under the Mafia's thumb until I snapped or until they killed me.

"It's not your fault," Eros snaps. His voice is sharp but his words... His words are— I don't know. It's like my brain has been put into overdrive and I think so anymore.

He moves to sit on the couch too, on the other side of me. He sits so close I can practically feel the jean fabric of his pants on my cheek. He's leaning back on the couch but his legs are lax and spread right next to me. His energy mixes with Kohen's and I melt a bit between them.

I knew I wanted them both, but in this moment, this tension solidified it. I can't just have Kohen. I need Kohen *and* Eros, together. Is that weird? Could I have them both?

"Yeah, it's not," I say, though the words don't even sound believable to me. How could I not get myself out of this? I'm a fucking serial killer for christ's sake.

"I want it to hurt." Kohen's words are the opposite of Eros. His voice is calm, soothing even, but his words, his eyes, are drenched in malice. His gray-brown eyes have more brown in them now, as the fire in front of him lights his face in a warm glow.

"We start from the bottom up?" Eros asks Kohen. When Kohen nods his head, Eros sighs. I can't help the smile that blooms across my face as I go to hi-five Kohen.

"I love when people agree with me," I say, curling into Kohen's legs as I stare at Eros.

"Yeah yeah." Eros waves off but sits with his hands clasped over his stomach. He smiles too, though. He's relaxed now, but I know a predator when I see one. He's excited too. For now we have a reason to kill.

Heading to class after brainstorming for most of the night on how to kill the entire Mafia is off-putting. I'm not looking over my shoulder, but instincts tell me I should be. Even though we haven't done anything yet.

The mere words "killing the Mafia" haunt me. As if the task isn't something I've thought of before. A task that has never been more real than it is now.

I take a deep breath as I go to my business class. It's Business 101 of sorts. I can't remember the name, not that it matters. Once Marcel dies, so does my tuition for schooling.

Stepping into class, on time this time, the chairs here look far more comfortable than the stools in the cooking class I share with Kohen and Eros.

My skirt is still just as short but this time I have on tights, so my cheeks won't touch the seat thank God. Sliding into a random row I find a woman, she's maybe a little older than me based on her mature aura, in a slick back bun and a cozy matching set. A cute brown sweater with pants made of the same material.

"Where did you get your outfit?" I ask as I sit beside her. She jumps about half a mile and her head darts up at me with wide eyes.

It takes her a second to process my words before smiling. She sets down her pencil, before peaking down at her outfit and back at me.

Okay, so while her outfit is incredibly cute, I don't know if I'd ever wear something that covered me completely like that. I love skin, sue me. I just needed a conversation starter.

"It's from a cute boutique downtown Litchfort. It even has pockets," she says and slides her hands in them to show me.

"Color me impressed," I say, smiling wider now that she's talking to me. These interactions go one of two ways. Once they start talking to me and we hit it off. Two, they ignore me or, even worse, insult me and then I'm imagining them hanging by their wrists in my art studio.

I don't take rejection well.

As much as I love killing, I've yet to kill a woman. I'm a girl's girl at heart. There also hasn't been a woman who's irked me enough to want to kill them, so really it's not a bias.

Men irk me much easier. I mean, all they have to do most of the time is open their mouths and I'm ready to jab my pencil in the sides of their necks.

That is, except for my lovely handsome man, Kohen... Eros, though, for Eros, I'd rather stick my pencil up his ass and even then he might like it. Hell, I might like it.

"Yeah, it's really comfortable," she says and looks back at her laptop.

"Wait, uh we should go sometime." Am I securing a girl friend here? Will this one stick?

"Uh," she hesitates and my face drops. Aww man. I purse my lips, trying to think of a way to salvage this.

Something tells me we are meant to be friends.

"Or we could do something else?" I suggest, leaving it open to her. Maybe she's more shy than I thought.

"Yeah," she lights up and I think I won her over. "We could—wait, no shopping sounds fun. We should go shopping," she says and it seems like she says it more to herself than anything, but I can roll with that.

"Perfect, I'm Pandora," I introduce myself, pulling my phone out to get her number.

"I'm Juliet." She smiles and tells me her number instead of typing it in.

"You a first year?"

"Yeah, I'm here for business," she says. Her shoulders relax and I'm sure I just made a friend. Is that the smartest thing since the Mafia is hot on my ass? No. But I might as well make the use of going to college, right?

"I'm a painting major. Why business?"

"I'm starting my own business. I make soap."

"Oh my god, you make soap? Stop, that's so cool. Can I try some?" I ask, scooting my desk closer. She leans down into her bag and hands me a yellow bar of soap covered in plastic wrap. "You don't need college. You're already a business woman, keeping your product on you, smart."

"I keep vanilla on me, but you look like more of a passion fruit kind of girl." My head shoots up to her and I smile.

"Yeah, but I know someone who likes vanilla." Kohen comes to mind. He is *so* a vanilla scents kind of guy.

"What kind of painting do you do?" Juliet asks and I scoff a bit. No one ever asks what kind of painting they assume or maybe don't care.

"Ahh well, I like to do dreamy landscapes and forest animals, paintings that look like they could've been made a century ago with a splash of pastel colors.

"Do you plan to sell? Can I see?" She tucks an invisible hair behind her ear as she leans closer to me, an action I don't think she realizes she's doing but I take the bait anyway.

"I do, I do now, but it's pretty slow," I shrug, showing her pictures on my phone. Phones never do it justice, but it's nice to have something to show.

The professor walks in and starts the class. I watch the clock more than I do the professor, but lectures are never fun and I've accepted that. As much as I should be trying to learn, maybe help grow my business so my Dad doesn't have to work as often, but I can't help the racing thoughts in my head.

Kill the Mafia.

Kill the Mafia with Kohen and Eros.

Keep the Mafia away from Kohen.

I sigh, damn this is gonna be a lot of fucking work. I skim over the rest of the student's here. I fail to find one of Marcel's minions here, but I can't let my guard down.

Not now when I have a plan. Or the semblance of a plan.

Soon, the class is dismissed and I stand, waving bye to my new friend and walking out of class. The moment I step into the hallway, I bump into a hard chest. The pecks on this one are fucking phenomenal and I know then it's not Marcel or one of his damn goons.

Brown eyes and tan skin field into my view. Shit. It's Eros, and sliding my gaze to the right, Kohen's here too. I step away faster than needed and glare back at Eros.

"You mind moving, you big oaf, people are trying to walk," I say, pressing a hand to his well-muscled chest and attempting to push him, or at least guide the idiot, out of my way, but he doesn't move.

"You should watch where you're going, Princess."

"Why are you guys even here? Is this your next class?" I ask.

"We're here for you!" Kohen pipes up and my tension melts away at his voice. He's here with us. He's safe here with us. "We wanted to walk you to your next class."

"*He* wanted to walk you to your next class." Eros corrects with a one-sided smile. "What do you have to say about that?"

"How sweet of you, Kohen," I say, turning my attention to my sweet man. Sliding over to him and linking one of my arms with his and leaning my head on his shoulder.

I guide him to my next class, oil painting, when I stop in my tracks. My arm around Kohen tenses as Eros runs into us from behind.

"What the hell." I hear Eros's voice, but I can't process anything beyond the man coming toward us. My bruise may be covered under layers of makeup, but it swells in his presence.

Kohen and Eros quickly pick up on who exactly is coming our way by the way Kohen's grip on me tightens and Eros flanks my side.

"Hi Dollface," Marcel's grating voice practically slaps me as he reaches for me. I see his hand and for a moment I wonder what would happen if I stayed between Ko and Eros. If I embarrassed Marcel by rejecting his advance so publicly. Would this temporary win be worth the plan?

"Hey." My voice comes out softer than I wanted. I reluctantly slip out of Kohen's grip. His fingertips almost don't let me go.

He fights letting me go for a split hair of a second. A second I hope Marcel doesn't catch."

I carry the ghost of Kohen's fingertips on my hand as I step away.

I'm strong. I've killed men the size of Marcel. I shouldn't be scared, but those are all planned. With weapons and drugs and more supplies than I could ever need. Those kills are different. They are for fun.

This is survival. The risk is more than just getting caught. If I don't successfully complete this kill, I'm dead. My Dad is dead.

I offer Marcel my hand, but he opts for my forearm and tugs me to his side. I catch Eros's arm following me out the side of my eye and whatever stopped his arm, I'm grateful for it.

I could get away with being with Kohen. He's part of my assignment from the Mafia. Eros, though, Eros is a big red sign I'm cheating, and the Mafia hates cheaters. At least those who cheat against them.

"Who are your friends? Introduce me," Marcel demands. His rough voice skidding across my cheek as he tucks me into his side. Slinging his heavy arm over my shoulders.

"This is Kohen, and Eros. We have a group project together." I keep it short, my fuse winding down as the reality of my situation settles in.

Marcel has me trapped.

"Nice to meet you guys. Hey it's about noon, let's go have lunch. You guys wanna join?"

"I have class," I try to find a way out of lunch. Absolutely no fucking way do I want to have lunch with Marcel, but lunch with Marcel, Eros, and Kohen? No. Hell no.

"You can miss a class I pay for," Marcel says, bopping my nose. Bopping my fucking nose. Like a dog. My cheek twitches and I try to keep the smile I know I can't let drop in front of an audience.

His neck in my view, all I see is supple clean skin that calls to me, his pulse calm and uninterrupted, urging me to stick a knife I don't have into it in front of all these people.

"That would be awesome, Pandora, you never told me you had a boyfriend," Eros says while Kohen goes stone silent.

"She didn't? Well, hopefully she didn't forget about me." His voice has an edge that sets me on fire to run, but I keep my forced smile anyway.

"Of course not, baby."

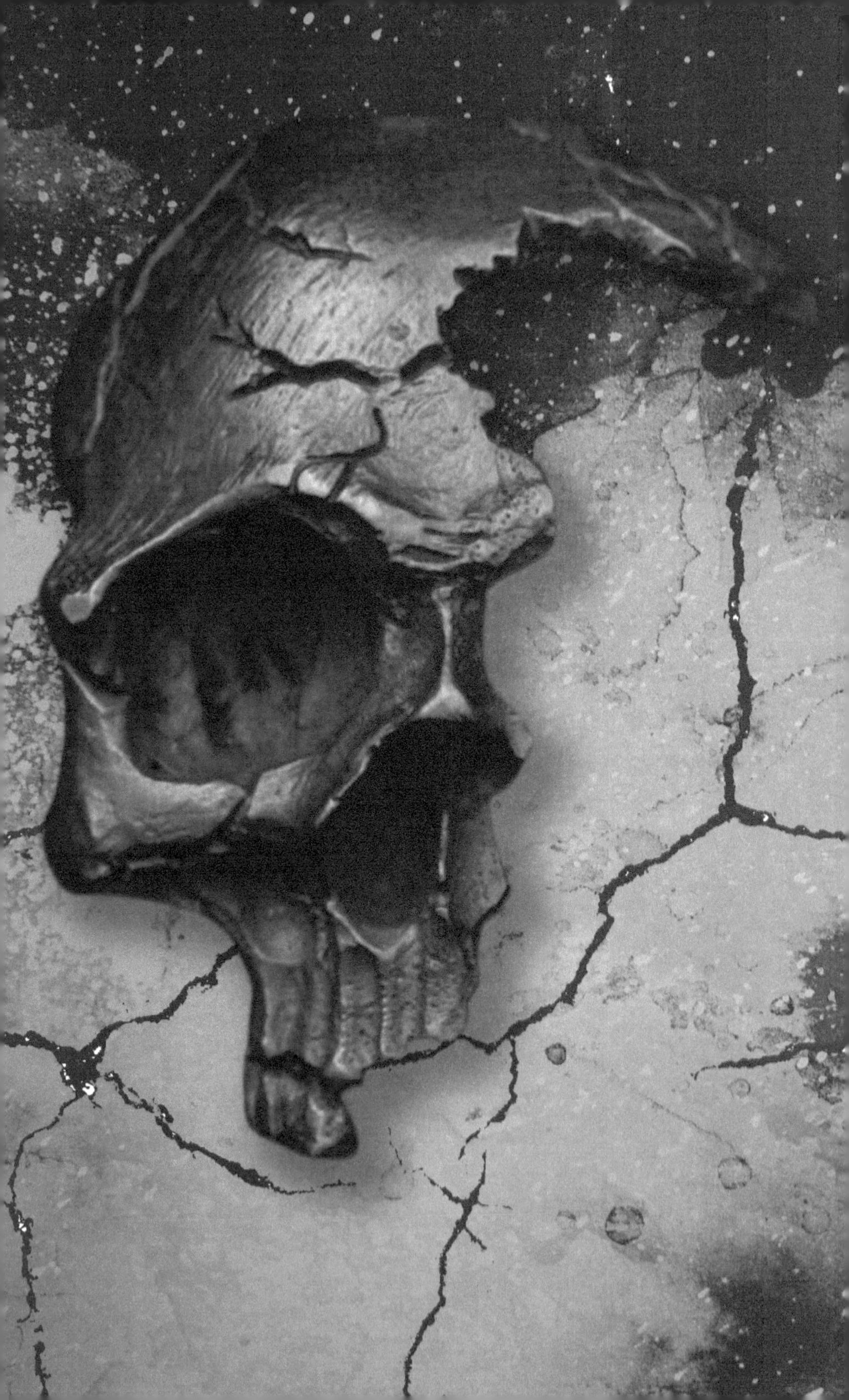

CHAPTER 8

Eros

I know we discussed leaving Marcel second to last in our kill order, but every time I see the fucker's face, he shoots up to number one for me.

Having a prissy ass lunch in a Mafia owned bar filled to the brim with Mafia members doesn't scare me as much as seeing Pandora walk towards the fucker she has to call "boyfriend".

We sit in a dark red booth with her across from Kohen and Marcel's ugly mug across from me.

The bar is decorated in red, as if the Mafia has no fucking taste. Red picnic patterned tablecloths with deep red curtains hanging off the two windows in this whole establishment. Brown tables and chairs fill the middle of the room with a bar on one side and a row of booths on the other.

"So, how did you two meet? Are you close?" Marcel asks, pointing his fork between Kohen and I. I hold back my scoff and throw a quick gaze to Kohen.

He's as emotionless as ever. His face gives nothing away to the naked eye, but I see the storm brewing inside. I see his winter facade trembling at the storm that bleeds through his skin. He's pissed.

As am I, but we have a part to play and a plan. I watch his eyes trained on Marcel, his eyes tracking his hands, waiting for a moment he might attack. We know Marcel is aggressive and we are on his turf. But striking now would ruin his and Pandora's little plan.

"Kohen's my boyfriend." Marcel's face scrunch up.

"You're gay?" Marcel says and I hear Pandora scoff. The tiniest smile on her lips is everything I need to keep going.

"Yeah, you got a problem with that?" I could fight the man across from me and probably five others. Kohen could easily do five as well, more if he had his gun on him. Which he fucking should. I told him to bring it with him at all times. I know Pandora is smart enough to get the hell out of dodge, so that's not a concern.

The thing is, if I can easily access my gun, so can Marcel. Marcel could easily grab his gun and blow Pandora's fucking brains out if I'm not fast enough.

"No," Marcel says, appearing to fight the twitch in the face. His gaze switches to Pandora with a raised brow, and she only offers him a small shrug.

"So, Kohen, it's Kohen right?" Marcel asks as if he doesn't already fucking know. "How long have you known my Dollface?"

Hmm, so he's not the stupid piece of shit on earth. He can sniff our interest a mile away probably, though I'm not too worried about it. I know we aren't the first guys to take an interest in the Princess. As much as the thought lights a simmer of anger in my gut, she's not the kind of girl to fall under the radar.

"We met in our cooking class." Kohen's voice is deadpan and he doesn't make eye contact with Marcel. His bloodlust is probably written all in those beautiful eyes of his.

"How long ago was that?"

"If you pay for the classes, wouldn't you know? I don't take you to be financially illiterate." Kohen snaps and Pandora's head darts to him and for the first time I spot worry in her eyes. Her brows furrow and she frowns.

I don't fucking like when she frowns.

"It's been—" Pandora attempts to answer. She even plasters that fake ass smile of hers that guys fall for all the damn time.

"I wasn't askin' you," Marcel snaps at her then turns back to his drink. She bits the inside of her cheek and her nails dig into her arm, which is crossed over her chest.

"Can I get you something to eat?" The waiter comes to our table, interrupting the silence that's growing.

"I'll get my usual and she'll get the house salad," Marcel orders first and, of course, even his ordering pisses me off.

"And fries, she'll get fries too," I interrupt. No fucking way this bitch orders Pandora a fucking house salad and that's fucking it.

"And a strawberry milkshake." Kohen pipes in.

"Okay," the waiter mumbles, then looks at me. I order a cheeseburger and Kohen gets a turkey club.

"It'll be out shortly." The waiter is quick to walk away. A piping hot Marcel would turn an average joe away, but not me, not us.

"What do you do Marcel? Are you in school?" I ask, even though I don't fucking care. I can feel my Society ring buzz against my finger for an assignment, but I can't leave Pandora, not with this prick.

"No, I help run the family business." He appears annoyed talking with me, but Kohen isn't saying shit to him, not today, not tomorrow, not ever.

"Family business of what?"

"You sure are fuckin' nosy."

"He's making conversation," Pandora tries to brush off, or excuse me, I don't know, but Marcel doesn't hear her, anyway.

Good. I want this bull trained on me.

"We're like a bank. We loan people money." Marcel lightly laughs at his piss poor description.

"Like a loan shark?" Kohen snaps. I turn my head to face him. When the hell did I become calm and him the storm? This isn't... this isn't right.

"Like getting people out of hard times when they make dumbass choices," Marcel snips back.

"Entailing?" Kohen asks, his bratty side coming out to play.

"Here's your food," the waiter quickly says, setting plates down in front of everyone. As good as my food smells, I look over to Pandora's dry ass salad and I'm pissed all over again.

"Doll, watch how much you eat–" Marcel is talking down to Pandora, he's whispering about her shape or what-fucking-ever and in the next moment, Kohen's butter knife is gone from his plate set and in the back of Marcel's hand.

A clean stab all the way through with the dullest knife in the universe. The bar goes silent. I'm watching Marcel to see if he'll fight back. Pandora gasps and Kohen is hard pressed, staring at Marcel.

Marcel's face is scrunched up in pain as his eyes glare at Kohen. Despite the pain, I guess the fear behind what his boss would do to him if he killed his prize is stronger than his need to get even.

"It's rude to talk about a woman's body at the table." Kohen doesn't look at Marcel. He blankly stares at something beyond us and it's almost scarier than if he was staring directly at the man. "Especially a woman as perfect as her."

"Duly noted." Marcel grimaces as he takes the dull spreading knife out of his hand. I'm partly shocked Kohen had enough precision and power to get such a dull knife to stick in Marcel's thick ass hand. Kohen picks up his food as if this lunch was moving along normally. Like it's perfectly normal to get a butter knife through someone's hand.

"I think I'll take this to go. Shall we get on with the group project?" I ask, pushing my burger away.

Pandora wordlessly nods as Marcel pressed a napkin to his hand. I see it's his dominant hand. My gaze catch's Kohen's profile. He's fighting a smirk and by god if I didn't think it'd put Pandora in deep shit, I'd laugh. That's what the bull fucking gets.

That's probably the hand he hit Pandora with.

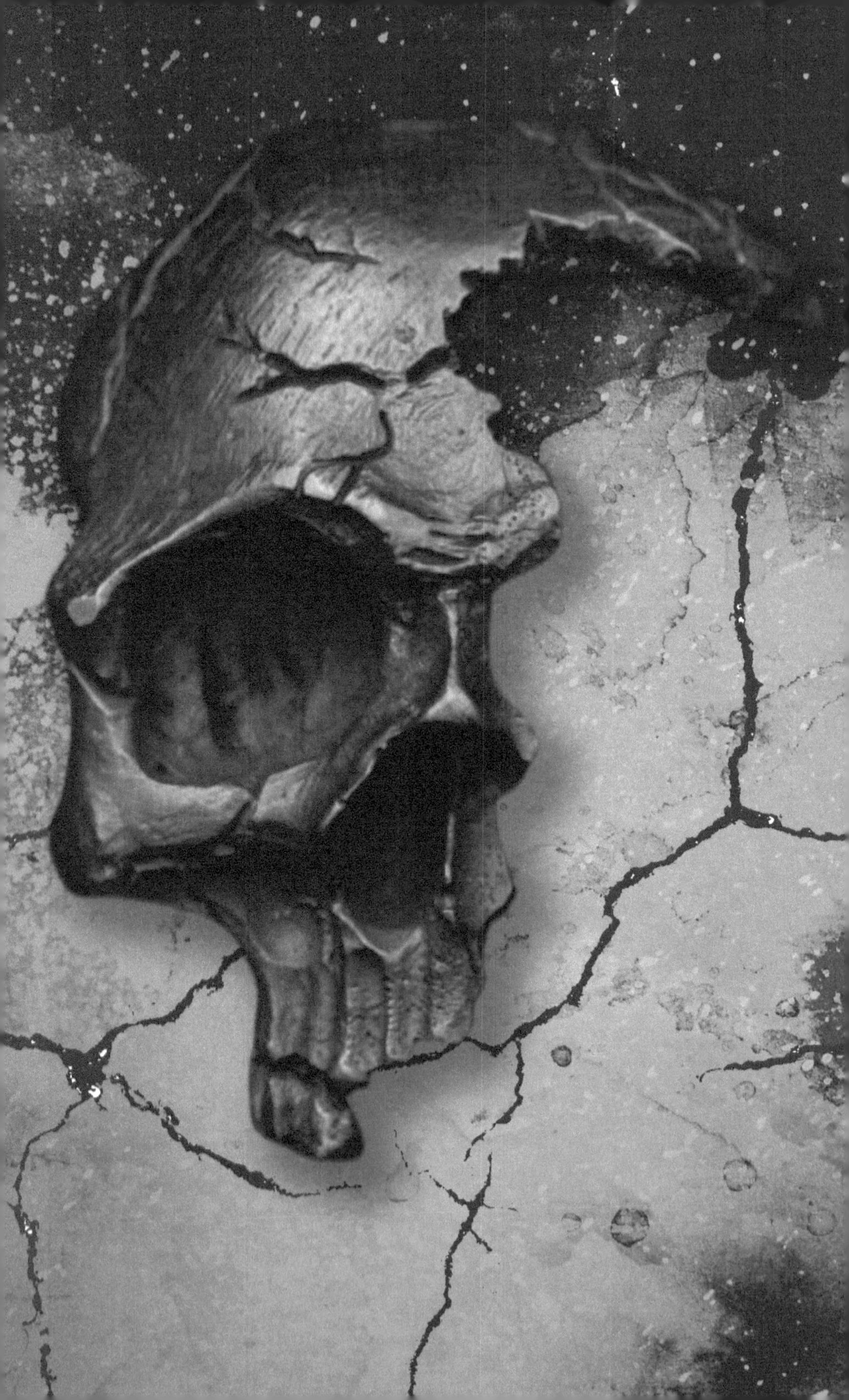

Chapter 9

Pandora

I'm half wishing this group project was an orgy cause holy fuck that was hot. I bite on my knuckles in Marcel's car as he drives me to Kohen's and Eros' house. They ride separately, of course.

Seeing the stab wound in Marcel's hand as he drives makes my ovaries ache, knowing that the mark was made by Kohen in my honor. In *my fucking honor*. Oh God.

And when they ordered me fries and a milkshake, which sits in the back of Marcel's car and will probably go uneaten, gosh, I was ready to slide under the table and blow them both off.

"He's got a fucking tongue and temper, doesn't he?" Marcel snips talking about Kohen. He's pissed, but who wouldn't be? At that moment I was glad it's Bruno, the Mafia Don, who wants Kohen and not Marcel because Marcel would've tried to kill Kohen for the disrespect.

"He's strong as shit, too. He's a hacker and a solider who would've fucking known," Marcel mumbles to himself, and I remain quiet.

A hacker? Since when was Kohen a hacker? Is that why they wanted him? I thought he was to replace Marcel as a right-hand man, but... was I wrong?

"All because stupid ass Panero needs help, now we need another one of those fucking hackers. Cocky pieces of shit." Panero is the hacker I know about. He's under the Mafia thumb as much as I am. His family is on the line, the same as mine.

I wanna ask why they need Kohen's help, but I know if I break him out of his trance now, he won't say. So I stay still.

"And you!" Fuck. "You sit there like a meek little–"

"Doll?" I supply, but apparently Marcel doesn't like that cause my head is slammed into the car window. He keeps one hand pushing my head into the window and the other on the steering wheel. My cheek stings with pain as my forehead throbs. Tears prick at my eyes, but I hold those suckers back. Ain't no way I'm letting a tear drop now.

The guy's house comes into view and Marcel pulls into the driveway.

"You better remember to keep your legs closed, you fucking slut, cause if I find out you're sleeping with either of those fuckers, Bruno won't be able to stop me from killing them.

I swallow a nervous breath. Little does he know how close I was to saying fuck it the other day in Kohen's bedroom. How close I am to saying fuck it once I get past their front door.

I instinctively use my nails to dig into his wound on his hand, forgetting I'm supposed to play the part of a dolce fuck doll.

His hand shoots back and I'm free for all of two seconds before metal slams into the side of my head.

"Why is it always a fucking fight with you? You want me to shoot you?" Marcel yells. I freeze, biting the inside of my cheek. Anyone is weak against a gun. The metal stings against my head, my hair doing shit all to cushion the hit.

Not that I thought it would, but it would've been nice.

"You hear me?" He yells again, shoving my head with the gun again.

"Okay!" I yell and he gives my head one final push before letting me go. He takes his gun away and unlocks the car so I can get the fuck out.

"Remember, get Kohen on our side. That's the only reason I'm letting you in alone. The fucker obviously doesn't like me. Use your girly appeals. Hopefully he's fucking bi or something," Marcel snips as I all bolt out of the damn car.

Thank god he didn't ask for a kiss like he normally does.

I attempt to smooth down my hair, but the guys are standing by their car already staring at me. They waited outside their car for me. How sweet.

How fucking embarrassing.

"What are we waiting for?" I ask as I come to a stop in front of them. I turn back to see Marcel's car pulling away.

"We should've killed him then." Kohen is the first to speak and it has me whipping my head towards him. His voice is still that rumbly tone that makes me want to drown in the words that he says, but I can hear the edge. The tittering tip of the cliff that threatens to fall and ruin everything.

"We have a plan," I sputter. His arm flexes and relaxes repeatedly as he considers his next words. The tension is practically written across his forehead and as much as I want to see him kill Marcel here and now, they deserve more pain than that. I deserve more. My Dad deserves true freedom and revenge.

"Plans change," He says calmly with a shrug.

"No, not this one. Eros tells him," I demand, hoping for once this man is on my side.

"I'm not telling him shit." Of fucking course not. Eros' jaw is locked hard and his eyes are set on Marcel's speeding away car. He's not happy either by that shit show, but honestly, when is the Eros not pissed off?

"Tell me, did I see a fucking gun?" Kohen asks, cocking his head. I leave his question unanswered and stomp towards their door.

"You guys have to be fucking kidding me, you have to be," I mutter as I turn around to see where they are.

Then suddenly they are right behind me. One reaching for the door and the other staring behind... keeping watch?

The warm air blasts me as we walk in. Kicking my heels off at the door, I wait for them to lead me to wherever.

"We have a plan, we have to stick to the—" I say, but it seems like my words are flown right into the void.

"Yeah, we heard you." Eros cuts me off.

"Well, did you listen?" I ask.

"Now that's debatable."

"We hit Lucas and Caleb, the Don's most trusted Caporegimes, tonight. Then Bishop and Noah, the consiglieres, the next up the chain of command, in two days." I say, rambling off the names.

"Then Samuel, the classmate, because he's closest to Marcel." Eros chuckles.

"Then Marcel and Bruno. Plain and simple." I finish. "We got this."

Eros heads for the kitchen and I follow. He takes his to-go container and pulls out his food. "Where's yours?"

"I left it in the car." I shrug as if I'm not freaking starving. I sit at the island across from where he's standing. Kohen slides onto a stool next to me. These bar stools are much nicer than any of the other stools I've sat on. These are covered in cloth.

"Here." Eros slides me his burger over the marble countertop.

"No, it's yours," I refuse, pushing the burger back to him.

"Now it's yours," he says and slides it back to me. I stare at the box, then back at him. Is he serious? "Do you want me to force feed you or are you gonna eat it on your own?"

Oh, he's dead serious.

Licking my lips, I pick up the burger, gosh that bar has some good burgers. I used to get them till one of Marcel's stupid ass minions mentioned something about getting fat. As if that's a bad thing. If he had two brain cells worth a shit, he'd know these burgers are worth being fat for.

My gaze flirts up to Eros, who watches me intently. I bite into the burger, staring at him and... and my cheeks aflame. Both sets of them. Setting the burger down, I wipe the side of my lips feeling ketchup and mayo slathered there.

"Thanks," I mutter, trying to look away from his intense stare.

"Another," he says. His demand is soft and yet still there. I meet his eyes and furrow my brows.

"What?" I ask, unable to control the amount of shock leaking from my voice.

"Another bite," Kohen sensually whispers in my ear. His head is so close to mine. His words land right in my ear. Is he trying to fuck my ear cause it's working.

I battle on whether to argue or give in. I should argue, I really should, but I'm hungry.

I pick up the burger again, my long nails gripping the burger as I bring it back to my lips. Before I bite I eye Eros again. "Are you sure?"

"Absolutely positive Princess." His gaze never leaves mine as I bite down again. Gosh, this is a good fucking burger. Even more so with an audience.

I clench my thighs together as I swallow. Fuck. Has it been that long since I've been fucked? So long eating a burger would turn me on.

If I'm being honest, it's not the burger doing it for me, but the whole damn meal.

"Now be a good girl and finish it," Kohen rasps. I don't see his face. His breath hits my neck and I lean my head in instinctively. His breath almost reaches down my chest and shit, I wish it would. When did eating a burger get so hot?

I arch my back and my hips tilt instinctively against the bar stool, wishing for some friction. Shit. I'm not even hungry anymore. My breasts are taught, tight with need. Their eyes, their fucking eyes on me like this. I can't handle it.

I bite and chew. This burger is good, but not what I want anymore.

Eros leans over the island. The island isn't wide enough to keep his piercing gaze from shooting straight to my core.

"Now Swallow."

Something about Eros bossing me around makes me want to disobey. For a second, I damn near spit the food out on the countertop, but for some unidentifiable reason, I listen. I swallow.

"The Princess *can* listen," Eros baits, and I glare past the lust I'm sure is all over my face.

"Ha ha," I sarcastically snip. Setting the burger back into its to-go box, I lick my lips. It takes everything in my damn soul not to wriggle on this damn stool. Silence falls over us as I stare at the burger, cause God forbid I reach either of their eyes.

"You have some on your face." Kohen breaks the silence. "Let me get that for you."

Instead of his finger, I feel his tongue swiping at the corner of my lips. My eyes dart to Eros, whose heady gaze meets mine. His chest rises and falls with rapid breath, as I'm sure mine is as he watches us.

"Oh God." The words slip from my lips and that's all it takes before my chair is jerked back and I gasp. Lips are on mine as I'm dragged off my chair into Koehn's arms as his lips ravish mine. I inhale as I grab the sides of Kohen's face and press him closer, smashing my chest to his.

These damn lips I've been waiting to taste for over a year touch mine. His kiss is rushed, heated, as his lips explore mine. It fills my stomach with butterflies as I push against him. His cotton shirt rubs against my exposed skin. He grabs hold of one of my hiked legs and presses his body further into me.

That's when I guess Eros decides to join our party cause he swoops in behind me. His front against my back as his nose finds my neck. His smooth brown hair grazes my neck. I hear him inhale as he nuzzles his nose into me.

"Such a filthy Princess—smells so damn good," He murmurs, pressing light kisses along my neck. His kisses get harder and harder as he reaches my jaw, and that's when I feel his teeth bite into my jaw.

"Not as filthy as you," I say between Kohen's kisses. I take one of my hands from Kohen and reach out for Eros.

His hand finds mine and instead of joining me from behind, he whips me around to face him. He steps away and the cold air rushes in, attempting to clear my mind. Kohen's arms snake around my middle as he attacks my neck with kisses and bites. I moan as he chuckles against me.

"With all your damn arguing, I'd never thought I was part of the deal," Eros says, raising his eyebrows. Kohen stops but doesn't move his arms from my waist.

I watch Eros. He stands there almost like a wounded puppy. His shoulders slump as his breath races, and I can still feel the ache in between my legs.

As much as the fucker gets on my nerves, he's always been part of the package.

At least, for me.

"Of course I want you too, dumbass," I say. "You've always been part of the deal." There is no Kohen without Eros and no Eros without Kohen. I want them both. I'm not naïve to think that either of them wants a painter who is indebted to the Mafia, so I'd never truly make the first move.

I find his hand again, and this time he holds it.

His calloused hand in mine as I pull him in. My gaze drops to his lips and he smashes his lips against mine. With his hands in my hair, he pulls me closer as Kohen's devious ass hands roam my body.

Eros's damn smirk comes through the kiss. I can feel the smirk against my lips. I scoff into the kiss.

"You can't help yourself, huh?" I murmur.

"Not when it comes to you, no." I'm up in the air and on the counter as both Eros and Kohen surround me. My chest rises heavily as Eros leans against Kohen.

"What are we gonna do with her, Ko?" His voice is light, mocking me, as I wither on the cool kitchen island. The burger is long forgotten as I watch them pose by my legs.

"Hmmm well, we've got options," Kohen says, his fingers tracing lightly up and down my leg, each round getting closer and closer to my core.

I can feel myself dripping in my panties. It's safe to fucking say I want them both now. Like right now.

"Fuck the options," I say and I lean forward and grab Kohen by his shirt. "You won't need this, and you won't need yours either." I nod towards Eros to take his off too.

Both are extremely lean, muscled. Their work for the Society pays off well in their bodies. Eros has muscles for fucking days and Kohen does too, though not as defined.

With Kohen's shirt gone, I attack his lips, needing a taste before I yank him down on the counter and swing one of my legs over him so I'm straddling him.

His hands catch my ass and I smile, accomplished with myself. Now we all can have the fun.

Flipping my hair over my shoulder, I look over at Eros. "Do you need an invitation or?"

"Your sassy ass comments are gonna earn you a spanking," He says, smiling as he covers my back, sandwiching me between them.

"You promise?" He scoffs as his hands explore my back. I grind against Kohen's hard on. Fuck, I forgot about my own damn clothes.

"I promise," Eros whispers as he tears my shirt down the middle in the back.

"That was my favorite shirt, you ass," I say, though it wasn't.

He chuckles and I feel his breath hit my back. Of course he doesn't feel bad, he doesn't give a shit.

"Then you should've taken it off, Princess."

I hear Eros grunt and Kohen lift me up by my ass as I collapse on his chest. I kiss his lips before I realize what's happening.

Oh shit.

"Eros!" I yell as I feel his fingers dig into my tights from the backs of my thighs, ripping them.

"You don't need these either." His mouth meets the skin of my thighs with kisses and nips, and I can't help but rock back into his touch.

"Fuck," I moan.

"Fuck indeed," Kohen murmurs as he jerks me up further up. My hands catch myself, landing beside his head as his hands remove my ripped shirt and unclasp my bra.

All I can do is watch and feel as they ravish my body with their lips. Kohen takes a free aching breast into his mouth. Sucking and nipping me as I moan.

He covers my breast in his saliva and the need to chase the high building in my body runs rampant. I grind my core against him.

"God Pandora," Kohen moans, meeting my hips thrust for thrust.

Eros lifts my hips and slides my skirt, panties, and the rest of my tights off my legs. His fingers find my throbbing pussy. His fingers curl inside me, teasing me, pulling me. He moves so slowly.

And each frustrated moan is caught by my sweet Kohen. His tongue fights against mine. He's such a fighter underneath his sweet exterior.

"This is the meal I've been fucking waiting for," He says adding his tongue and I want to fucking scream. He licks his tongue flat against me and I shudder over Kohen. Pressing my head into his forehead, I kiss him as Eros eats my pussy.

I'm so close. Between the grinding against Kohen and Eros eating me out, I don't know how much longer I will last.

"Come on Princess, feed me," Eros demands. His breath hitting my pussy lips. The constant battle between rock against Kohen and riding Eros's face is too much. The pressure is practically choking me. My air comes out in choppy segments as I burst, having had all I can take. Shit. I bit onto Kohen's shoulder in a lame attempt to ground myself, as I'm sure I'm staining his pants.

Well, I would be is Eros wasn't still lapping at my pussy like the good fucking dog he is.

I sit up, causing Eros to stop, and he quickly takes up the space at my back and looks over my shoulder. Kohen's hard under me and I cock my head to the side as I stare at my pretty man.

"I think it's time for your reward, Ko," I say, tracing a light finger down his chest.

"I agree," Eros chuckles.

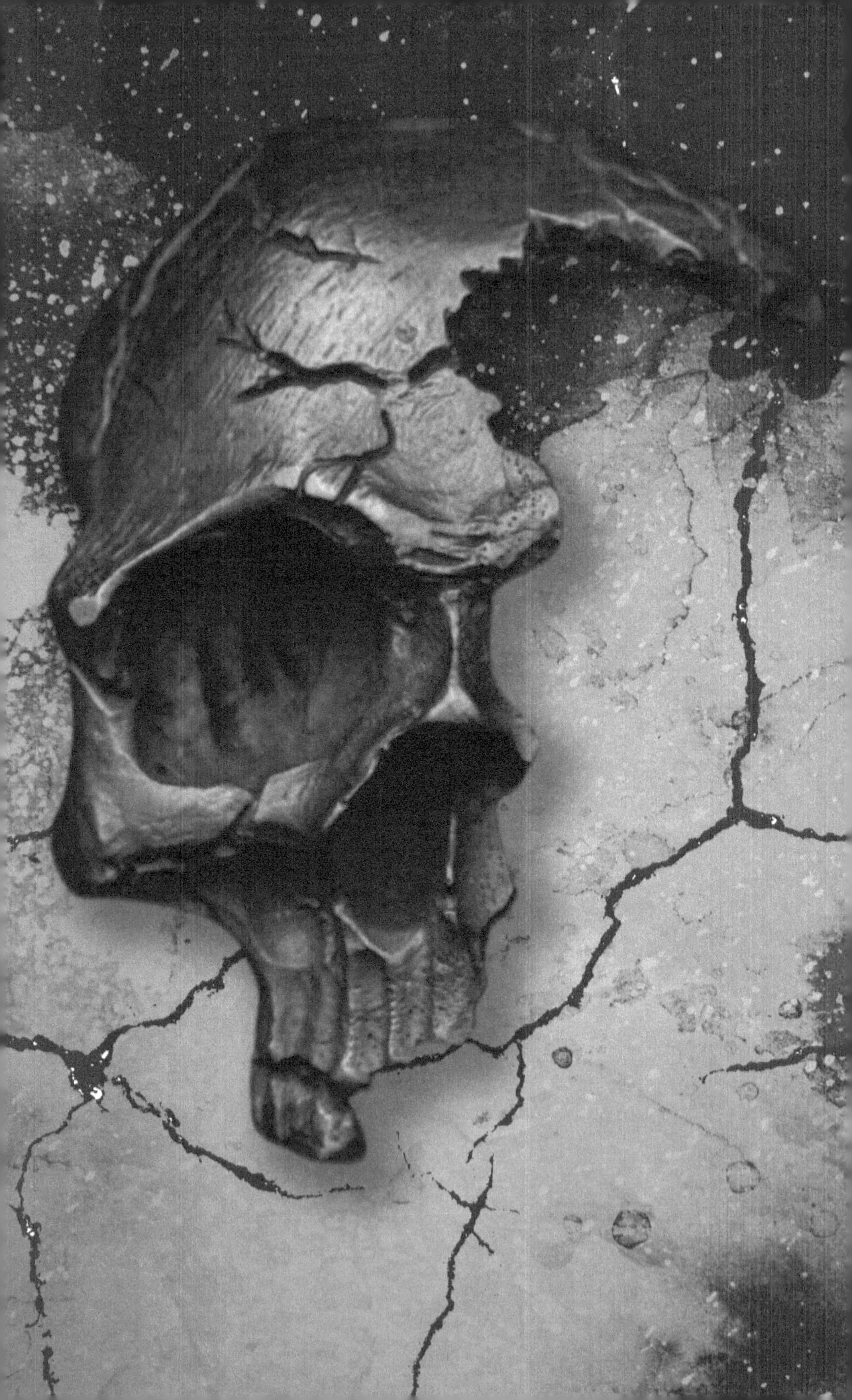

Chapter 10

Kohen

"It's okay–" The words sputter out of my mouth faster than I can comprehend. Pandora straddles me, her pussy directly against my cock, lightly wetting my pants, and I can't tell if it's her cum or Eros saliva. Either way, I'm about a thousand times harder than I was watching her eat that fucking burger.

"You've got two readily available, more than willing hopefuls wanting to pounce you baby and you're gonna say no?" Eros asks, creasing his brows in a fake concern. The charmer has a way with words I'll never be able to beat.

His face is covered in Pandora's cum and it's so fucking hot I can only stare at him for so long before I come in my fucking pants.

"No–" I say, trying to get the right words out, I gulp and Pandora watches my throat intently as I am staring at them. I'm confused, conflicted and hard. "I mean, if you–"

"It's not just about me, sweet man," Pandora says. "We wanna take care of you, will you let us?" Fuck.

"Yes," I say in anticipation. Shit, it was never supposed to get this far. We were never supposed to be together, and yet here we are. Here they are. Here we are. Together. "Please fucking yes."

"Of course, Ko, let us take care of you," Eros murmurs as his hands wrap around Pandora's waist and lift her body hovering over me. "Now drop your pants, baby."

Lifting my hips, I follow orders. My cock brushes along Pandora's pussy and has us both moaning out.

"Good." Eros says with a light smile on his face. "So now, we might be ready, but we need to make sure the Princess is. Can you do that, Ko?"

My face flushes as I nod. Eros then wraps his hand roughly around Pandora's neck and pushes her toward me, and I capture her lips with mine. I fucking love the taste of her plump lips. The touch of them against mine. Her skin rubbing against mine, I let her bottom lip catch on my canine tooth.

"You're such a good kisser," she murmurs, rolling her body over mine and kissing me again. "Feel what you're doing to me."

She takes my hand in hers and guides me to cup her sex. She moans and I swear I commit the sound to memory. Shit. I love that sound. I find her clit desperate to hear the sound again, dipping my fingers in her, teasing her a bit. I love the way she bites me, nips at my skin when my fingertip barely enters her.

"You fucking–Ohm." She gasps as she jerks forward.

"I'm prepping your backdoor baby, you scared?"

"You wish," she snarls, pushing back on his hand and wincing.

"Seriously though, slowly Princess," Eros coats as he backs his arm away. I can't see his hand. "Don't hurt yourself."

I insert more of my finger and she rocks against my fingers as I pump, matching her rhythm.

"Wait," she says and I stop and I'm pretty sure Eros does. "I'm ready. I need you inside, both of you, please."

"As you wish," Eros says and looks at me with a smile, one I haven't seen a whole lot of recently. "Ride Ko first."

"My pleasure," she says and leans up, her breast round and heavy as she sits up. God, I need another taste. Yet I can't break her concentration, not this time.

She wraps her hands around my cock and my hips jut towards her. Fuck. So much for cool, calm and fucking collected. She pumps her hands swiping at the pre-cum at my tip and I swear I'm gonna blow, but before I do, she lines me up with her sentence and slides down in one swoop.

"Oh," she moans, squirming a bit as she gets comfortable. Her walls soak me up. Welcoming me as she sits.

"You feel fucking amazing," I breathe as she meets my eye. She leans over me like a predator and rolls her hips. Earning a moan from both of us.

"My turn, you ready Princess?" Eros asked. He's got sweat on his brow and his throat is all veiny from concentration. It's a fucking vision seeing them both.

"Ready," she confirms. I can slowly feel him inch in her through her walls. She's clenching and unclenching as I'm sure the sensations build. Both pain and pleasure, and I'm more than fucking ready for all of us to become one.

"Oh fuck," she whispers against my chest. Her whole body shivers and it worries me this may be too much.

"Are you okay? It's okay if—"

"If only I knew we'd be like this," she says, kissing my chest. My chest blooms with warmth, knowing she loves this, loving us, and I nod towards Eros.

He smirks as he pulls out and thrusts forward, rocking her onto me. Fuck. "Pull back at the same as I do Princess," He instructs and soon we're finding our rhythm, back and forth and creating a mountain of pleasure I've never felt before.

"Please." The words from my lips and I don't even know what I'm begging for. I'm so fucking close.

"We got you baby," Eros's voice brings me back and I stare at my knight and princess. His hand reaches out for me, and I grasp it. We each have a hand on Pandora's hip.

His thrusts don't let up as our moans and grunts mix in the air. He's zoned in as his eyes are half lidded and he's cursing.

He becomes erratic with his motion and soon I'm coming into Pandora and she's coming on me. Her walls grip me as Eros rides out our orgasms and I can't help the fear they'll slip away from me now that we're done.

Instead of separating, Eros lies on Pandora, squishing her between us. He glances at me, giving me a small nod before closing his eyes and cuddling us.

"Knock the wind out of you, big boy?" Pandora says as she snuggles against my chest too and I sigh a breath of relief.

"Shut the fuck up before I stuff your mouth with something else," Eros grumbles.

"Can you even get it up again?"

"You sure wanna test that theory right now Princess cause we sure fucking can?"

"Shut up," she mutters. Her lashes flutter against my chest and I close my eyes, enjoying the weight of both of them on me. Wrapping my arms around the both of them, I relax fully as Eros draws random shapes on my skin.

I can breathe easy knowing they aren't planning to leave me.

At least not so soon.

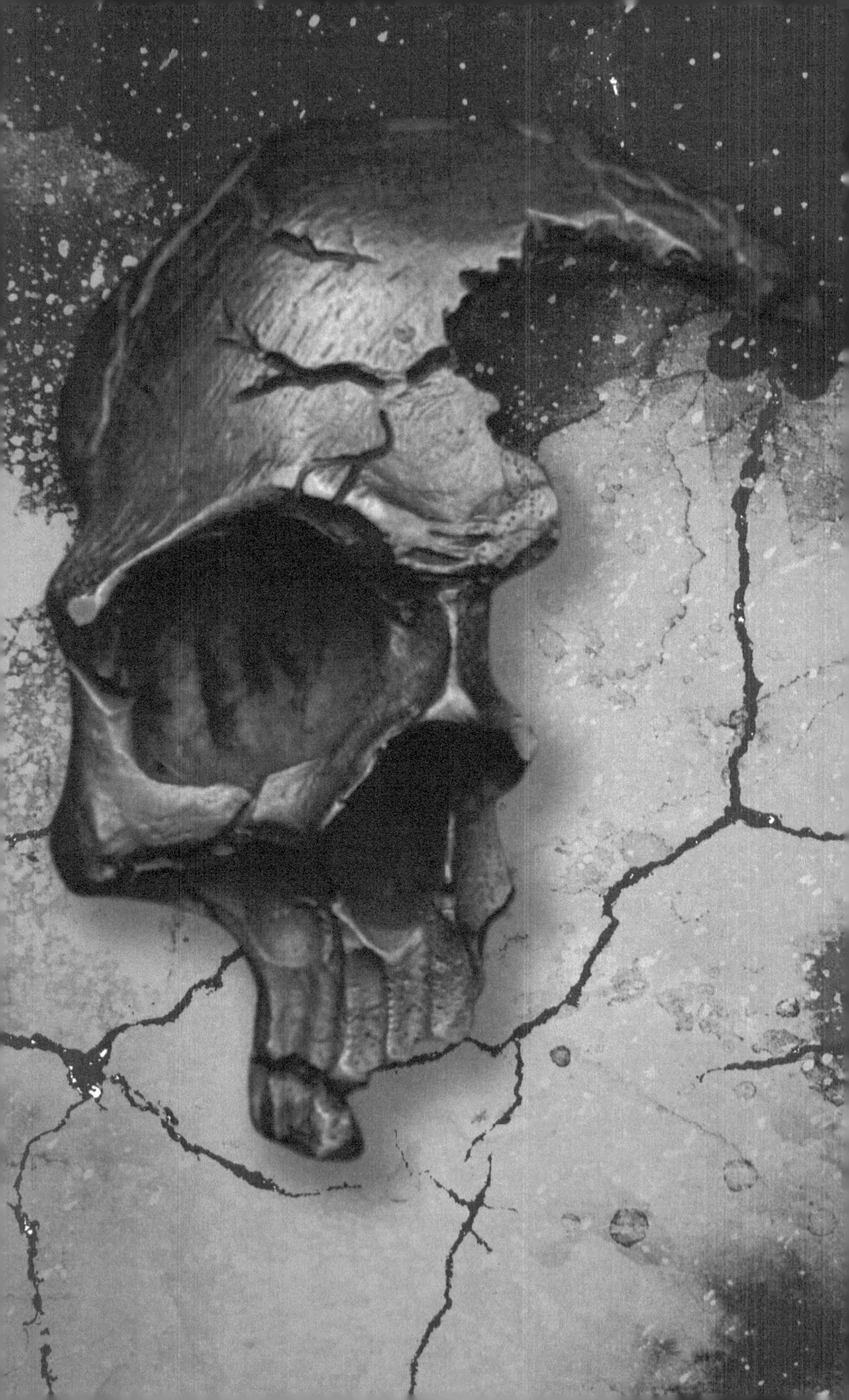

Chapter 11

Kohen

I kissed her. I actually kissed her. More than that, I fucked her. Well, Eros fucked her while she was fucking me, but all in all, we were together. As a whole, a unit, and I loved it.

The ride to our first kill had a warmth filling in under my skin. It's the three of us, together again. I love this emotion in my chest. It comes every time we are all together and it's stronger than before.

I crave it. I taste the lingering aftertaste in my mouth and I need more of it all the time.

"Ko, I want you to stay in the car," Eros says.

"Absolutely not," I say, turning to Eros. I see Pandora in the backseat watching us intently, and I wish I could know what was going through her head. Does she agree with him? Do they want to go off without me?

"Why Eros?" Pandora asks. She scotches up the seat, popping her head in the middle of us. "I thought all Society workers are trained the same."

"I'm used to killing people. You're a literal serial killer, but Ko, you're not comfortable killing people, and that's what we need to do tonight."

"I've killed Eros," I argue, even though I know what he means. I've killed, but more than that, it's easy. It's easy to kill and morally. I've struggled with accepting that. It shouldn't be easy. It should weigh on you. I should *care,* but I don't. I care more about the fact that I don't care.

Every time I kill, I'm reminded of the fact that I'm not normal. Eros tracks his kills. As most guards and serial killers around us do, they care. They enjoy it even. I get nothing.

I *feel* nothing. I can't count my kills because I can't bring myself to care.

It's not normal.

"Wait, how did the Society find you if you're not comfortable being a killer?" Pandora asks as she stares at me. She scrunches her cute eyebrows and I have half the nerve to kiss the space between them. My lack of care is probably why the Society recruited me.

They must have known, somehow.

I sigh, moving to gaze out the window. I don't have the most grandiose sob story as to why the Society recruited me. Still, pain rings in my chest as I think about it.

"I grew up in the system, no birth parents, no adopted parents. I jumped between homes and one day on my way home I stumbled into a higher up Courier. He recruited me, gave me a home in exchange for my devotion to the Society."

"So you don't have to be a member? How old were you?"

"No, I was 14, I grew up in the Society. They saved me," I say, though my words can't compel the weight needed. The Society saved me from a horrible life in the system, from bullying and abuse, and gave me the skills I needed to live. Gave me Eros and put Pandora in my life. I owe my life to my higher ups.

That's why I stay, even though I don't want to. I dream of a different life. A life away from the Society. A life with a family I build for myself. How fucking selfish is that?

"I want Ko with us," Pandora says as she stares at Eros. He grumbles and rolls his eyes.

"What if he gets hurt?"

"He won't. He'll be safe with both of us there. Please, he's capable. This involves him too," Pandora pleads.

It's nice not to be the only one fighting Eros. Though, I hope he doesn't get offended. Wait- Eros is stronger than that. I shake my head, trying to clear my thoughts.

"You have your gun?" Eros asks. I take it from my hostler on my waist and show him. He nods as grunts as we pull into the alley beside the warehouse with our targets inside. "Okay, you can come, but you listen to us. I can't live if something happens to you. Physically, or mentally."

"I know." Those it's hard to remember under all the self doubt that racks my brain. As much as he can't bear the thought of me getting hurt, I'd protect him, them, with my last dying breath so I don't know why he bothers trying to hold me back.

They are mine. Both of them. It's about time I acted like it.

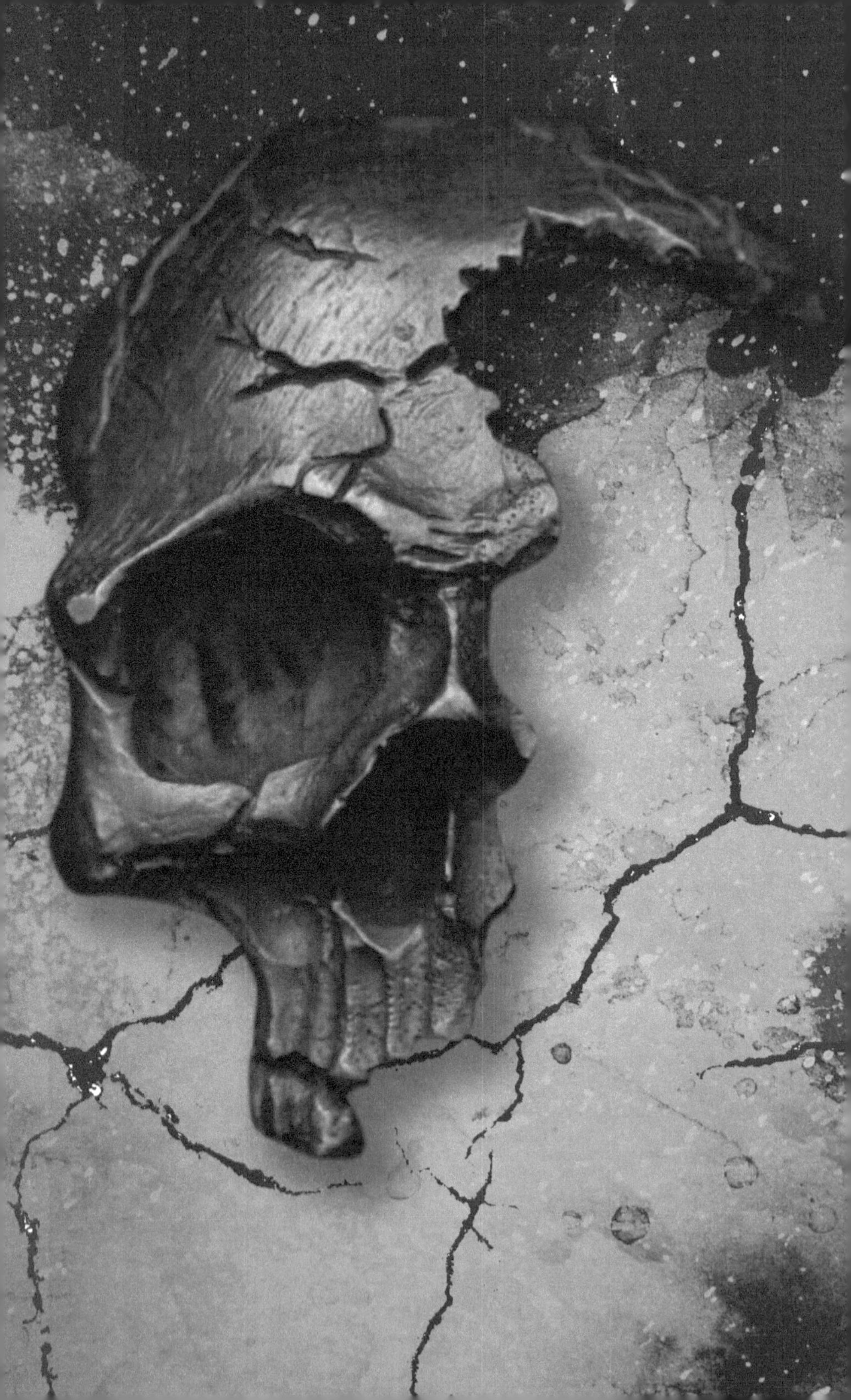

CHAPTER 12

Eros

I don't stand a fucking chance against Kohen, and adding Pandora to the mix has made that so much more impossible.

"Wait, before we go inside, can I have a gun?" Pandora asks, poking her head into the front seat area of the car.

"Like I have extra?" I snort.

"Please," she begs and pouts her fucking lips and shit. When did saying no become so difficult?

"Do you even know how to use one?"

"Of course," she says. I can't tell if the damn Princess is lying or not. She gazes at me with those brown eyes and I find myself slipping the gun from my glove box, because yes I have a spare, into her hands.

I'm so gonna regret this.

"Show me how you hold it," I say, turning to face her.

She only smiles and holds the gun with both hands. She aims out the front windshield, not at one of us, thank God, and slides the safety off.

"I had training when I started killing people," she rambles as she clicks the safety back on and studies the gun.

"By who?" I ask. Jealousy coursing in my veins as I imagine some dumbass instructor with their arms around her.

"At the local gun range, duh," she says, rolling her eyes and sliding out of the car. Kohen and I quickly follow suit.

Kohen holds his gun in his hands as we approach and I try to banish my worry for them both away. Distractions are a sure way to end up making a mistake. A mistake that could cost *them.*

The warehouse they stay in is an abandoned one on Elmore street with bars over the windows and rotting wood for the exterior. Rain and grass permanent the air as we approach. We can hear two idiots speaking loudly about takeout inside.

Slipping in the door, Pandora takes the lead, gun drawn at her side. Though we let her lead, we are hot on her ass. She doesn't go far without us.

Soldiers stand right by the door and I take a knife, silently stabbing through their necks, blood hitting my chin as I carefully drop them to the floor. No need to hint to Lucas and Caleb they are under attack.

Kohen is on the other soldier, setting him down on the floor.

"How nice of my little guard dogs. Big doberman energy guys," Pandora whispers as she struts forward.

Pandora's a killer, this I know, but in the face of death, she's so cold like it's a normal Monday for her and my knee jerk reaction is to be... turned on. Of fucking course.

The warehouse is made up of narrow hallways and dark corners with more men that we waste no time killing. Pandora takes her stab at it, letting their heavy bodies plop on the floor.

"Don't make too much noise," I whisper, raising my brows at her. She has the audacity to roll her pretty eyes at me.

"Don't be boring Eros," she says, walking to our last set of doors. According to the map, this is where the main room is, which means whatever trade is happening tonight will be in here. Lucky for us, no one else will be here for three more hours.

Their drugs will find a building of dead bodies.

"Yeah, don't be boring," Kohen mocks as he follows her.

"Pandora? What are you doing here?" the one named Lucas asks, not noticing her gun. Lucas has brown hair and tanned skin, like most of the Mafia here. He's about five foot eleven and wears a worn out leather jacket, which gives me the impression it either has sentimental meaning or the Mafia doesn't pay him as much as he pretends with the fake designer belt he proudly wears.

Lucas is a Caporegime, meaning he's a captain of a division within the Mafia. He's in charge of the money and controls about 50 soldiers. Caleb, who has yet to show himself, is a Caporegime too, instead of money he's put on product management. Anything going in and out is on him to oversee.

"Hey Lucas," Pandora says sweetly as Kohen and Eros step out of her shadow.

"What the fuck? Caleb!" He shouts as he sees our guns. That moment he calls Caleb, a gunshot rings out. I turn around, but

Kohen's faster. His gun is already trained on Caleb and he's shooting him, a bullet going straight into Caleb's forehead.

His body slumps over the railing and hits the ground with a crunch. If I wasn't so fucking used to the sound, I'd flinch.

"Ko, you made that way too easy, babe," Pandora complains.

"We still have Lucas," Kohen says and turns to aim his gun back at Lucas, who is standing frozen in his spot.

"Hmm, true," she says, suddenly satisfied.

"Pandora, go fucking home." Lucas spits as he aims his gun at her. Aims his gun at her. This fucker aims his gun at what's mine.

I move instantly. My training from the Society comes in fiercely as I run to Lucas before he has time to register his next move. I'm on him faster than he can move his gun to point at me. I jut my arm out and hit his wrist, causing his grip on the gun to weaken. Before he has the chance to pull the trigger in panic, I take his gun, throwing it off to the side.

Stomping his calf, he's down one leg. He falls to his knees and, for good measure, I swing my arm and pistol whip him. Next time he aims a gun at what's mine, I want him to think of the cold metal of my gun slapping across his face. He slams down on the floor and I shoot a bullet right in the middle of his right thigh before his pleas register in my ears.

"Wait, wait please," Lucas cries out as he lands on the floor. Jerking him up by the front of his jacket, I slam him down into a random chair. A fold up chair on the verge of crumbling under his body weight being slammed down on it.

"Let's talk," I say, finding some zip ties in a drawer in his desk off to the side of the room. I tie both his hands to the chair, though if he wasn't crying his ass off, he could probably break the chair and move freely.

"I don't know anything. All I know is the drop is here tonight, whatever you're mad about-"

"We're not Mafia and you fuckin' know it," Kohen spits as he stares down at Lucas. His eyes are more brown than gray. His snarl isn't as obvious as mine, but I can see the up tick of his upper lip. Kohen's beyond pissed.

Lucas' gaze switches between us, then lands on Pandora. I watch his face contort. He's confused. Sure. I mean, they didn't know about my Princess. Not this side of her. And now they get to pay the price of that.

"Pandora, what the hell?" Lucas yells. As if he has room to be the one asking the questions.

"Don't 'what the hell me', you know what's up," she snips. "I'm here because of my father and your greedy ass hands on my boyfriend."

Kohen's head snaps towards her and so does mine. I watch as she leans down, pulling a paintbrush from her back pocket and dipping it in the blood spilling from Lucas's leg. She paints his cheek as she sighs, and Lucas moans in pain.

"Why does the Mafia want Ko?"

"Ko?" He gasps in pain as the nickname slips from his lips. Pandora nods toward Kohen, who's moved to be as close to her as I am. Standing over her, ready to pull her back in the event Lucas lunges.

"When did the Mafia spot him? And why?" I ask. My eyes tick over to the clock above us. The pick up crew won't be here for another hour, but something in my gut is churning.

"I ain't tellin' you shit," the deadman spits even though he already has a bullet in his right leg. Pandora shrugs and stabs her paintbrush into his bullet wound, pressing it in deeper than I thought a paintbrush could go.

Lucas screams as tears roll down his eyes in fat drops. His body shakes in pain and I think he might drop dead.

"When he accessed Pandora's school files—we needed a hacker, a hacker." His words come out rushed but we heard them. Pandora's head whips over to Kohen, who has the nerve to blush.

Pandora goes back to painting Lucas's exposed skin as she thinks about his words. "So it's not my fault?"

"Of course not, it's mine. I hacked into the University's system to find out what classes you were in," Kohen mumbles as if that's the only thing he's hacked into to find information about her.

He humbly forgot about the surveillance cameras of any store she walks into, the campus's camera, hell the man snooped in the Society's files to find absolutely anything he can on her. Social media pages weren't enough for my little Ko.

"Oh Ko," she says sweetly, turning her best smile towards him. "I knew we were meant to be."

"Let me go, please, I won't tell Marcel, I swear."

"You don't have to worry about Marcel," I say, my blood boiling at the fucker's name.

"You don't know what he's capable of–"

"He doesn't know what we are capable of, obviously," Pandora murmurs, sliding her brush from Lucas's forehead to his chin and down his neck. His skin is covered in red as his face swells from the hits I landed on him. Blood, tears and snot drip all over him, and he looks horrifying.

"One more thing," she says, stepping away from him. She stands with her arms behind her back. "Why do you need a hacker?"

He sighs as if it's getting hard to breathe, and it probably is. The man was shot and has lost a lot of blood. His face is pale and his breathing is slowing.

He's got minutes and I wonder if he knows it.

"Someone trying to take over the Mafia from the inside out. Bruno needs to stop him." This is news to me, and it must be news to Pandora cause she appears shocked. Her eyes widened and her shoulders straightened.

Someone is trying to take over the Mafia realm already, which means another person needs to be added to our hit list. A whole other person. Fuck.

"Who?" Kohen asks, but Lucas shrugs, weakly shaking his head. His breathing is slowing and we have minutes to try to get a name from him.

"Who, Lucas?" I snap, stepping forward and aiming my gun at him again. Fuck, we are running out of time. His eyes appear darker now.

"Please, help me," He whimpers and that's when Pandora pulls the gun I gave her from her waistband. The sound of her clicking off the safety alerts Lucas to her movements.

Before he can beg again, she shoots him between the eyes and he slumps over.

"Pandora, what the fuck, we needed to get a name," I shout. She's completely motionless. Her lips are straight and her skin even appears a bit pale, a grayish sheen, and my anger turns into worry. Does she already know?

"Anyone hungry?" She asks as she shrugs and leaves his body to slop out of the chair. Lucas's body hitting the ground with a thumb.

Two men down, seven more to go. Eight more to go, actually.

"What the hell–" I say, but Kohen cuts my words off by grabbing Pandora's hand and walking away from the crime scene.

What the hell am I going to do with these two?

"Guys, we can't ignore there is another person added to the mix," I say, following behind them. "Do you have an idea?–"

"No, I don't, but I know Lucas didn't either. He wouldn't have. Bruno isn't dumb enough to let his name be spread around. Only one person would know the name, and that is Bruno himself."

She reaches a hand out to me. I eye her hand, what ifs running rampant in my mind.

They aren't worried enough. Not as much as I need them to be. I need–

"Come on Eros," Kohen's warm voice reaches my ears and I snap back to reality. I grab the Princess's hand and she squeezes and her lips wear the smallest smile.

"On to the next," she says, pulling us both through the warehouse.

On to the next, I guess.

CHAPTER 13

Pandora

The adrenaline has worn off by morning, but fear has set so deep into my bones I can't hardly sit still. I stopped trying to do my makeup after messing up my eyeliner for the third time.

"You'll be okay." Kohen's voice makes me jump from the black holes in mind as I twirl around to face him.

"You should be gone, both of you," I say as I stand in front of my closet. I reach for a skirt and tights, though all I want to wear is sweats. A hoodie will have to do.

"I couldn't leave," Kohen says, his big eyes filled with something I can't describe. I freeze mid-shimmy to get my tights up and I watch his fidgety hands and slouched posture. He's as worried as I. Why?

I scrunch my eyebrows as I walk to him, he's sitting up in my bed, and I grab both sides of his face, forcing his eyes to meet mine head on.

"What's wrong?"

"Nothing." he attempts to shake his head but I won't let him. His hands rest on my forearms but he isn't pushing me away, he's pulling me closer.

"Ko," I say. His name falling in the air between us. "Are you okay?"

"I knew this would happen," Eros says, sitting up from the bed and softly running his hands up and down Kohen's back. "It's too much. The kills are too much."

"It's not," Kohen argues.

"But it is."

"It's not and that's the problem, Eros. It's not normal. I'm not normal. It should bother me that I can take someone's life and it doesn't."

"It doesn't bother me either," I say. "It never has. I'm sure it doesn't bother Eros either. That's why we're meant to be together," I say, kissing the top of his nose and smiling. I try to be reassuring though it's hard to mask with them. It's not that I don't want to mask around them, it's that I'm so comfortable that I physically can't.

"We're meant to be," Ko says like he's convincing himself, but whatever will catch him up to speed with me, I'll take.

"You should be feeling bad about questioning if you deserve our love, not about the lack of emotion around killing people. You're ours, don't you know that?"

"He feels guilty about that too," Eros says, laying back down.

"It's okay to feel guilty about... not... feeling guilty about killing someone. I do it all the time," I shrug. I wish I could be more helpful to my sweet man, but I—this isn't something I have experience with.

"Okay," He murmurs and swoops me into his lap for a proper kiss. His soft pillowy lips meet mine and by a Goddess herself, thank goodness I get to taste him in this lifetime.

I attack his face with kisses, his nose, lips, cheeks, forehead, any inch I can reach. His smile, his chuckles, they are all mine.

"Can I get one?" Eros's deep voice asks as he leans back up.

"Oh my God, you *can* ask. What a good boy," I say with mock shock as I lean over, still in Kohen's lap, and meet Eros waiting lips.

"Little one?" A knock at the door has me scrambling off Kohen's lap. As much as I am grown, that is still my Dad.

"Yeah," I yell through the door. He never opens my door and always waits for me to open it.

"Uh, your ride is here." His voice waivers as he speaks and I look towards the guys. Eros is already up with his gun drawn and Kohen is close behind him.

"My ride?" I mutter. My ride…. Marcel? "Um yeah, here I come."

I open my door slightly, a crack so my dad can't see the guys or the gun. I look around him, hoping I don't find any weapons pointed at him.

"Dad, are you okay?"

"Yeah, it's just—It's not Marcel at the door."

"Who is it?" I ask.

"One of his guys, I don't know which." It takes everything not to face my guys. Did the Mafia already find the bodies? I was sure it'd take them at least until lunch. According to their schedule, Lucas and Caleb aren't supposed to check in until lunch.

"Okay, yeah, I'll be down," I say and pull my dad closer so I can whisper. "Is he in the house?"

"No, he's sitting in his car. Are you gonna be okay, Little one?"

"Don't worry, we won't have to deal with this too much longer," I say. He scrunches his eyebrows and shakes his head, but I give him a kiss on his cheek and turn back into my room.

As I bend down to grab the handle of my bag, I slightly shake my head no, letting the guys know everything is okay.

Not that I know if everything is okay, but at least, I hope it is.

"Who is picking you up?" Eros whispers, moving to stare out the window. I don't answer since my Dad is still at my door and I don't want him to know I have men in my room. I half shrug as I sling my bag on my back. I make eye contact with them both, one after the other. Hoping they can read my eyes.

We have to play along. We have a plan, and we need to stick to it.

Shutting my bedroom door, I turn to face my dad whose wrinkles have only gotten deeper and his frown more and more prominent.

"Dad, um," I say, kind of clueless on what to say. "I love you."

This earns me an upward tick of his lip, something I would've missed if I wasn't paying attention. I smile, the full smile I was hoping to get from him, but maybe one day soon, I'll be able to see it.

"I love you too, Little one. Your Mom would've been so proud of you," He says then quickly turns around thinking I didn't see the way his eyes glass over.

Walking out the front door, I refrain from looking back at my bedroom window. I know they are still there. I can't believe I'm leaving two Society members in my bedroom with my... with my Dad.

Wait. Why the hell haven't, I thought of this before? The Society could help me, could've helped me. I have three get out of jail cards and I could've used one for my dad, put protection details on him while I kill the Mafia.

Wait–that's fucking brilliant.

"Hurry the fuck up Pandora, I don't get paid enough for this," I hear Marcel's goon yell from the car.

"Oh shut the hell up." I scoff, sliding into his car. Samuel, my surprise classmate, sits behind the wheel and by the looks of it, he's the only one in the car. Good, cause it's small as shit. Flipping down the mirror, I apply lip gloss as he pulls off. "What's up with the chauffeur act?"

"I ain't your damn chauffeur barbie," He spits. "I'm only following orders."

"From who?" I ask, keeping my tone light. Pulling out my phone, I pull up the group text with Eros and Kohen, send them a text of the car and driver, though I don't have the license's plate. It's probably fake anyway.

"Marcel said you were fucking nosy." Their texts swarm in with questions I can't answer.

> Pandora: I need to cash in one of my Society cards, get security details on my dad.

> Eros: where the fuck are you going?

> Pandora: Don't leave my dad till he's protected.

> Kohen: pls be careful, we're coming.

> Pandora: don't bother, he's taking me to class.

I see bubbles pop up, but they go away. I wonder if they believe me. I wouldn't if I were them. And that's the problem. I need them to protect my Dad. I can handle myself from here.

"Why isn't your master here today?" I ask. The question both let me in on what's going on but also piss Samuel off. A win win.

"I thought he tamed your foul ass?" He murmurs, spiting out the window like a fucking slob. I internally cringe at the sight, but a dog can't help but be... well... a dog.

"Thought wrong, now speak," I say, hoping the demand works since casual conversation didn't. I need to know why he's here.

"I ain't your damn dog."

"You wanna be?" I say, a sly smile covering my shiny lips as I turn to face Samuel. "I treat my dogs so well."

He hesitates, his eyes leering at me, before shaking his head. "Marcel would kill me."

"He doesn't have to know."

"He will. Marcel knows everything."

"Like what?" I ask. He's shaking his head like he's hearing voices or something, his fingers twitching and he's on the edge of his seat...away from me.

"Wouldn't you like to fucking know," He sneers

and I give up, sighing as I lean back, letting my head roll on the headrest.

"You taking me to class?" I ask.

"We have a stop to make first."

"Where?" I ask. A chill settles over my bones. A break in patterns is never a good fucking sign. I knew and yet, I resisted it. I probably signed my death certificate getting into this damn car.

"You'll see," he says with a lame ass shrug that tells me absolutely nothing.

Fuck.

"Dollface, you truly disappoint me." Marcel's eagerness to see me has him waiting out by the sidewalk like a valet and despite his attitude, I take my time getting out of the car. He slams the door shut behind me and drags me with a hand around my throat so our faces are mere inches apart.

It's not as hot as when Kohen does it.

"What's the matter, honey?" I ask, feigning innocence.

He raises both his eyebrows and scoffs and he drags me, by my fucking throat, to the front door of his house.

To be honest, I can't tell if he's mad about me killing his men, or for something else I could have possibly done.

I don't know, I've been pretty good, besides the … killing part. Maybe I missed a date or something?

Not that I'd have to worry about those for much longer.

The minute we are through the door, I'm thrown on the cold marble flooring. I guess for a secondhand man, Marcel truly does make good money. Hard ass flooring makes for a less than ideal landing and my arm throbs with pain.

My high heels scrape against the floor and I nearly wince hearing the leather get ruined. I've never been to Marcel's house. It's always been warehouses and bars where he parades me around.

My vision blurs all the porcelain angels and stone naked babies in his entryway. It's nice from a man's perspective, but gaudy and ugly all at the same time. All this money and he couldn't hire an interior designer?

"What the fuck?" I mutter as I attempt to get up from the floor. I get to all fours before a damning kick puts me back down. My chin nearly knocks into the floor and I squeeze my eyes shut. Fuck. Nothing could soften a blow to the stomach from a man who has about 100 pounds on me.

I stay on the ground, too breathless and hurt to get up. Turning over on my side, I huff, my hand clutching over my stomach, the damn bastard.

"Fucking bitch, what the hell?" I curse as he bends at his waist, peering over me. I watch as Samuel and Noah, consiglieres of the Mafia, stand behind Marcel like his little soldiers and the sight of them standing there doing nothing pisses me off royally.

Marcel isn't done with me yet. His hand lands a blow over my already bruised cheek and I spit blood onto his white, shiny floor.

My face burns and I'm sure my makeup is ruined, but I stare up at Marcel anyway. As much as I want to cower, I can't.

I'm stronger than this. I have to be.

"Next word out of your mouth better be an explanation of why we found two dead bodies this morning?"

Well, fuck.

"What makes you think I could take down two grown ass men?" I hiss. "I'm just a fucking girl." Marcel had to be fucking stupid. Who would think I, a dainty 5'4" girl, could kill two grown men.

I'd giggle if I could, cause I definitely have, but Marcel shouldn't know that. I was supposed to be the least likely suspect. The dead-ass *last* person who could have done this, so how does he know it was me?

"Where's Bruno? Did you let him in on your little failure? Two men dead on your fucking watch," I whisper in his face, which he didn't like. Not one bit, cause his gun is in my damn face again.

"You want me to turn your crazy ass into Bruno? Maybe show him the damn tapes?"

"Tapes of what?" I ask, blood draining from my face both internally and externally. Blood from my nose drips on the floor, but I don't think it's broken, thank fucking God. I have no idea how Eros and Kohen are going to react.

Maybe I should've told them to track me down.

"Tapes of you and the pretty boys killing Lucas and Caleb at the Novel Wearhouse last night." His smirk is beyond annoying. That was the warehouse we killed them at, but that's easy information if he found the bodies this morning. And Tapes? Yeah, I fucking doubt it.

"Prove it." I snarl.

"I don't have to prove shit to you." Bluff. Kohen would've whipped any cameras. He would've, right?

"I'm going to give you one chance. One singular chance to right your wrongs. You go to class, you act normally, as if we know nothing, and lure them to us. Both of them will take their punishments and yours." And I get away scoot fucking free? Yeah right.

"Then what?" I'm not fucking new.

"Then you move in here with me, as my personal fuckdoll, in exchange for your life. Now you owe *me*, Pandora, not just the Mafia. I saved your life, after all."

I look back at Samuel and Noah who stand like fucking statues behind Marcel, who's cackling like a damn cartoon villain. His shoes scuff on the marble. He steps back, losing his balance over laughing so hard. I watch his shoes as looking anywhere else is unbearable. I swallow the vomit, trying to come up. Or is that a sob? Either way, I focus on shoving that shit back down.

I wipe the blood off my lips. Well, fuck. There goes my plan.

"Samuel, take her to class," He says then turns back to face me. "And remember, we're fucking watching you."

Chapter 14

Eros

The damn girl doesn't know when to let us in. Good thing I don't need her permission to do shit.

"She's at Marcel's house," I say, staring down at the red dot on my phone. "You stay here with her Dad, I'll go get her."

It took us a minute too fucking long to track her phone, but we got her location... which is moving... right now?

"Stay with her Dad? The same Dad who doesn't know I'm here?" Kohen says and I stop in tracts as I load my gun into my holster on my waist.

"You're scared of her, Dad?"

"No," he says, crossing his arms. "I don't want our first meeting to be him finding me in his daughter's bedroom."

"It'll be okay, baby," I say and plop a kiss on his lips before climbing out Pandora's window. We have got to meet her Dad properly so I can use the front door.

My boots hit the ground and I run to my car. Parked a few houses down like we're fucking teenagers or something. Sliding in, I check the tracker and see it's moving again. This time... towards the school? Wait what?

That was a quick pit stop.

Looking up, I see men and women in society attire flood the sides of Pandora's house. I see my teammates, Guards from the Society, take position around the house. I nod toward them in acknowledgement as I see Kohen sneak out Pandora's bedroom window.

"The Guards are here," he says with a shrug as he jumps off the roof, landing beside me. I shake my head, but I can't muster up the energy to laugh. I head towards my car parked around the block and he follows. Something in my gut tells me even though she's going towards the school, something is off.

Something isn't right and I need to see her. I need to know she's okay.

Parking the car, Kohen and I slid towards the east building where our cooking class resided. Watching the red dot move on my phone, I'm anxious to see her. An itch that's spread from my gut washes over my body and I damn near sprint to find her, my Princess.

As I get to the door, I swing it open, the warm air covering my skin as I walk inside the school building. Brown hallways and clean-ish floors squeak under my rushed footsteps. Turning corners, I have Kohen hot on my heels.

The closer we get to the class, the closer we get to the red dot, the easier it gets to breathe. I look up from my phone and I see her, swaying her hips as she walks into class. I follow close behind her, leaning over her shoulder when I get close.

"Where the hell were you?" I whisper against the side of her head. She has her hood up and she doesn't turn towards me so I can see her face.

"Princess," I say and put my hand on her shoulder and whip her around. She smiles but... she has more makeup on than she did earlier. More of that same color shit. "Ima kill him."

I turn on my heel and move to leave the class. Fuck this class, fuck this plan, and fuck Marcel for landing a hand twice on my fucking girl. Twice is two, too many times.

"Eros no," she grabs my hoodie. I'd have to rip her hand off my hoodie to move, and I can't risk hurting her hand.

"Eros no, what?" Kohen's voice follows and he pauses when he sees her face.

"I'm a big girl."

"You're hurt, again." Kohen sounds about as hurt as she should be and it increases my need to kill this fucker.

"Please, my Dad..."

"The Society is there to protect him, so it's time," I say, trying to release her hand from my hoodie sleeve. Except she has the grip of a damn vice and I can't remove her hand without prying her off me.

"Our plan will make it hurt so much more. Death is too easy for the rest of the players here, Eros," Pandora whispers now, grabbing Kohen's hand and walking backwards to our desk. We are a considerable distance away from everyone since our kitchen station is in the back. I doubt anyone can hear us, but I see that Mafia asshole sitting at his own station.

His body language is tense, and his worry practically bleeds through his skin. He might as well take a sharpie to his damn forehead and write "I'm scared as shit". Is he in trouble with the Mafia? Or does he know he's on my fucking shit list?

I'll kill him too. I do it right fucking now if I could.

"What's up with Samuel?" I ask as I let her lead us to our stools. She sighs in relief as we sit and I can't help but feel the tiniest bit of pleasure seeing her smile, or her trying to smile. Even with a black eye and busted lip, she's still one of the most beautiful princesses I've seen. I guess we are participating in this class today.

Pandora relaxes as the professor starts blabbing. My stares meets the fucker with a countdown clock above his head. He sits under the classroom clock and it's fucking hilarious as I envision the clock striking the hour and my racing to kill his ass. He's bluntly watching her, and I narrow my eyes at the fucker.

Who the fuck does he think he's looking at?

My patience is wearing pretty fucking thin. I'm holding on to Pandora's thread of vengeance by its ends and it's fraying. My hand is slipping. One thing the Society has taught us growing up is that we don't lose.

In this world, there is no losing, there is only life and death and the Mafia has played their hand.

It's time I play mine.

I may have to deal with the Mafia on my own.

Pandora snaps her fingers in front of my face and I smirk as I stare at her. "Yes?" I ask.

She takes a deep breath as she slides off her stool. She grabs the dough from the mini fridge and that's when I realize I have no idea what the hell we are making today.

She unwraps the cling and leans in towards Kohen and I.

"They know, I don't know how, but they do," she whispers so low I can hardly hear her. It takes skill not to jerk my head in her direction. Not to lean in closer, because what the hell did she say?

"They know what?" I slowly ask. Kohen spreads flour over the dough and I noticed my hands covered in flour from leaning on the counter. Are we making bread?

"They know about last night," she murmurs, kneading the dough. She presses in and she slightly tilts her head in the direction of Samuel. I keep my jaw from hitting the damn floor.

"How?" I asked. Between Kohen and me, we should have been undetectable. We've been undoing this shit since we were 14. There is no way they have us on camera. There can't be.

"Oh shit, were there cameras?" Kohen asks and my eyes meet his.

"Cameras?" I ask. Wouldn't he know that? He should have known that. It was his job to take them out pre op. He's a Courier. Couriers are the ones who think about these kinds of things. Wiping cameras, delivering goods, deleting flies, cleaning crime scenes—that's their job.

But Kohen doesn't look surprised. He scrunches his eyebrows but that's forced and the fucker can't hide the upward twitch of the right side of his lip. He can't even fake his surprise.

I blink, as if stupid came and slapped me across the face. Kohen's never made mistakes. He's meticulous, annoyingly so. It's not just his job, but who he is. No. Kohen left the cameras on... on purpose.

Fuck. Why?

"So the video is real?" Pandora says, blood draining from her face.

"Ko," I say. I'm left speechless. My mind runs with a million possibilities of why Ko would leave us in a spot like this and I'm drawing a blank. What was the point? Why would he leave evidence? What would The Society think?

Do they already know?

"I forgot," Kohen shrugs and I shove him, covering his shirt in flour.

"No the fuck you did not." I say, and he has the nerve to laugh. Pandora's face is a mix of shock and hurt as she registers what I said.

"Kohen, you did that on purpose?" Pandora asks, scrunching her eyebrows.

"Anything to make it hurt more, right?" Kohen asks and Pandora looks away from him. Staring at the over kneaded dough on the counter.

"How does that hurt them more?" She whispers. I see the questions cross her mind. The load she carries becomes heavier and I almost want to knock Kohen upside his head. But I don't. If anything, he had a reason, a damn good reason. One we may not even be able to see.

"They're scared. Fear is a stronger monster than pain. Fear will eat them alive. Pain is temporary."

"Fear?" she mutters, confused.

"Fear, something that runs so deep into their core it'll affect their decision making, creating an opening for us. All they will be able to think about is when we will hit them next. Killing their henchmen instead of them outright will throw them off, as you placed, but knowing it was us will heighten the unknown for them. They'll be wondering if and when we'll snap again." Kohen smiles as he explains, gently taking the dough from under hands and putting it in a pan. He walks over to the oven to put it in and that's when Pandora breaks.

She lets out a laugh. Slowly, she looks up at me. Her lips spread into a creepy ass smile as she laughs again, cackling. Throwing her head back and her arm clutching her stomach. I see the slight winces from her body, but it doesn't stop her from laughing.

She turns on her heel and grabs Kohen by the front of his sweater and pulls in him for a rushed kiss. A bruising one, where her nails dig into him and her lips smash into his with excitement.

"You are a fucking genius." And this is when I'm reminded of who this woman is. Pandora Melrose. Pandora is not a meek mouse, or even a big growly bear.

She's a serial killer. The rush of a kill and the ruin of someone being something she's good enough at to be recruited by the most dangerous society of killers. She craves this kind of danger. And that's when I know she's for us. Without a shadow of a doubt.

I begin to realize I may be the most normal human in this little group. And I'm okay with that. I smile as my gaze meets Samuel's, who does nothing to help his group make their bread. I find the bread knife, the one with tiny dips with pointy tips on it. I bring it to my neck almost close enough to make a cut and make a motion to slice my neck, holding my gaze.

"I'll kill you personally," I mouth as he launches out of his chair, stumbling into the group member holding the bread pan. The bump causes the pan to drop and even as his group yells at him, Samuel doesn't break eye contact. Maybe he's too scared, maybe too aware I'll advance the minute he lets his guard down.

I'll be there when he does. I might be there sooner.

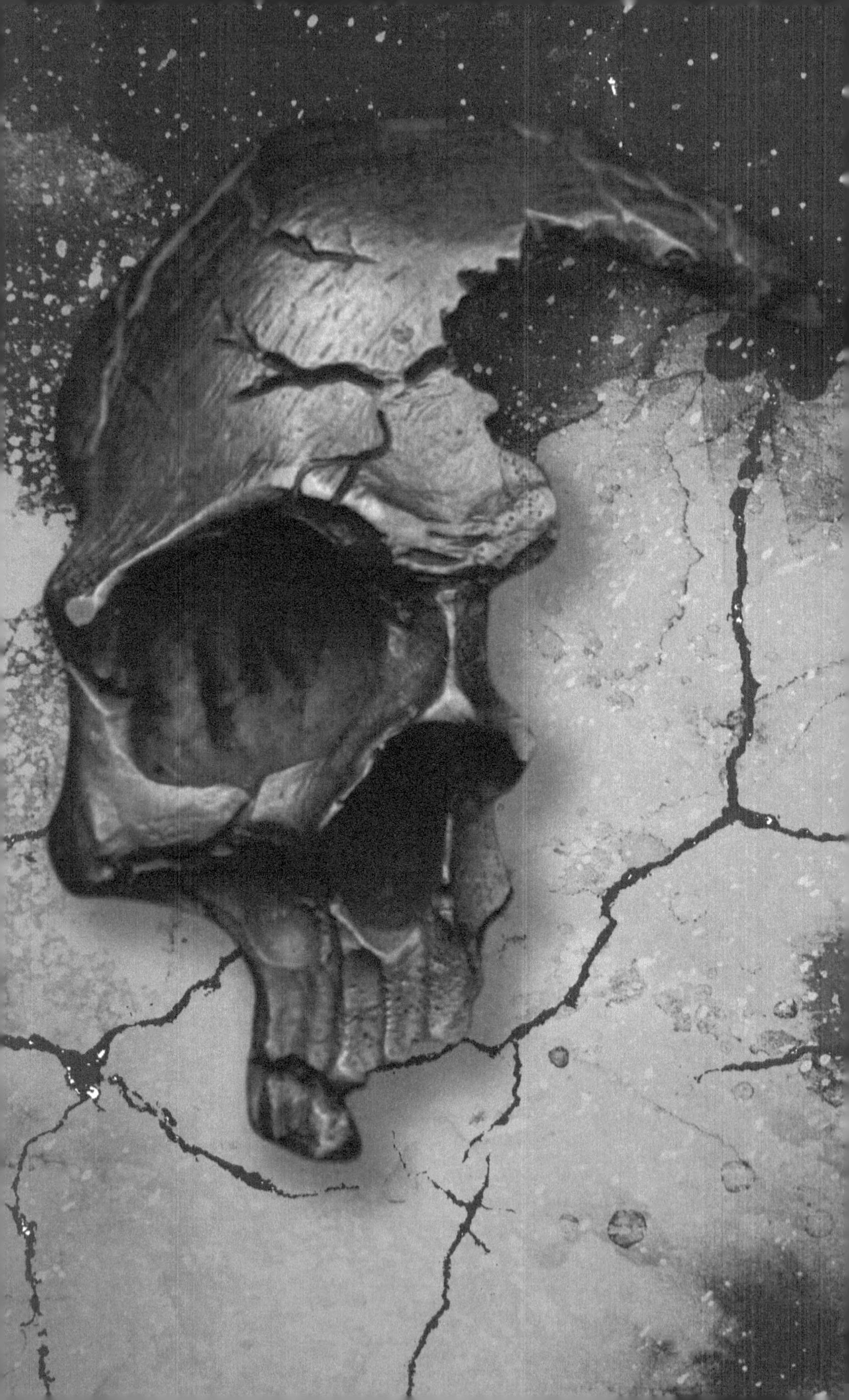

Chapter 15

Pandora

I'm losing my edge. I can feel it. There's something so deep, so essential to my being that I'm losing. I've been losing it for a while.

It started when I didn't kill the Mafia men for putting a gun to my father's head.

That moment changed everything.

Bruno Yearwood and Marcel Amos should be dead. They should have died that night.

And it's my fault they aren't. I let them live in fear I would lose something far greater than my own life.

Now the Mafia thinks they can offer me the same deal in a different envelope and I'd be dumb enough to accept.

They know I'm scared. They don't know the monster I used to be. The ruthless killer who didn't give a damn if the offense was a simple ass grab or a full on assault. The person who didn't feel. The girl who was never trapped in her own head.

They don't know her.

I don't know her. Not anymore.

Swallowing, I brush the paint onto my canvas and look around my studio. The lack of red in the room blares at me. It screams in my ears and they ring. The silence chilling over my heated skin.

I only use red when I kill.

It's been too long.

The deer on my canvas can't see me. Her eyes are glazed over and I know spiritually she can't see me. If she did, she'd cry. She'd cry at the sight of what I've become. When did I run at the sign of trouble?

My hand lazily splatters the acrylic and it spreads to the wrong spots, it drips all wrong, in the wrong spots, in the wrong consistency. I bite my cheek to hold my sobs back. The painting is ruined.

I stare at my mess on the canvas. *Something* has to give. This girl I've become is weak. Inconsolable, unsaveable.

I take a red dollop of paint and dip my brush in it. Painting a line on my forearm, I watch the red coat my skin. A thick layer covering half my arm.

I smile.

Weak, inconsolable, unsaveable.

Taking a broken wooden paintbrush, I stab the sharp wood into my arm. I relish in the pain that spreads. I don't go as deep as I normally do, but enough to get the blood to spill. My blood.

Taking the same paintbrush, I paint my arm with my spilling blood. Splatters stain my clothes, the desk, the floor. I don't care.

My exhales are much easier as the girl I've turned into dies.

I am Pandora Melrose, a member of Mortes Ostium, a serial killer and a lover. I can do anything. Be anything. *They* shouldn't have been able to trap me.

I let them and I can't anymore.

I move to my canvas, tears and blood pouring out of me as I fix my painting. This time red tears drip from the soft, delicate deer and the sadness in me starts to dissolve.

I am stronger than this.

My arm is completely red and the pain subsides as I finish my painting with red skies.

My Dad, Kohen, and Eros can't pay the price of my weakness.

I have to do this myself. I have to kill the Mafia by myself.

I need to tell them.

Rushing out of the studio, I run home. Feet pounding on the concrete of the sidewalk, little rocks poking me, kicking off my heels somewhere on the sidewalk, I run faster. My family's house comes into view and the smile on my lips hurts my cheeks. Whipping open the front door, I head straight to the kitchen where my Dad should be.

It's empty.

I race to the living room and he's not there. Maybe he's sleeping? I take the stairs two at a time and I get to his bedroom, only to find it empty. He's not here. Is he at work?

My phone dings and a video loads from... Bruno? Why is he texting me? He's never texted me before. I forgot I even had his number.

Waiting for the video load, I wash my arm, my hands and once the video file loads I dry my hands and hit play.

I nearly drop my phone at what the video contains. My Dad appears in a chair, in a dark room and Marcel is next to him with a bat. Fuck.

Am I too late?

His first swing hits me through the screen and I can't breathe again. My Dad doesn't yell out or cry, but by the bite of his cheek I can tell he wants to. He doesn't. Maybe he knows they were going to send this video to me.

Marcel swings again and I watch the entire two-minute video. My punishment for taking this long. For being late.

I rush to my room; I put on a black hoodie and leggings. Grabbing every knife I own and the gun I kept from Eros. I check the bullets like he taught me and I storm back out of the house.

I have time; I have to have time. I have to save my Dad. I have to kill the Mafia.

I have to kill them all.

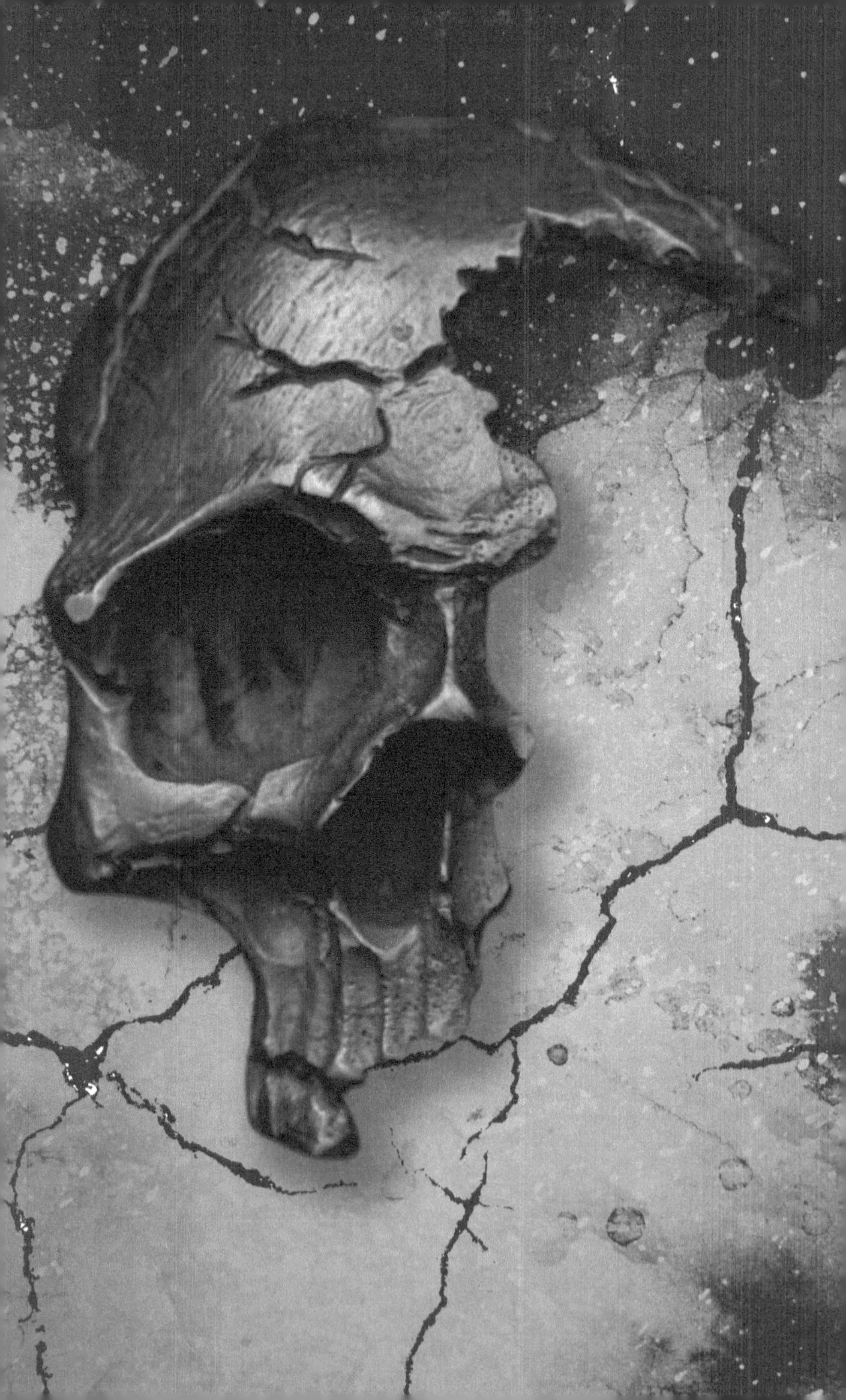

Chapter 16

Kohen

I shouldn't have let the video go through to her phone. It was selfish. A gentleman would have blocked it and went to save Mr. Melrose before she noticed he was missing. But my girl needed to see it. The cost of straying from who she is.

Eros and I purposely beat her here. We rushed to Bruno Yearwood's home where her Dad is. Having all three of our phones linked up, Eros and I got the text her Dad was here too.

I couldn't be more grateful I was fast enough to stop the video from going to her phone immediately. This all happened so fast, I'm not sure she's ready.

I met Pandora Melrose before she joined the Society, before I became her special Courier. Her obsession with me started way before my first delivery to her art studio.

Pandora is a killer. Always have been. The Society would have found her, eventually. I sped up the process by giving her the recommendation.

I'd swore to keep her at a distance. To not get emotional. The Society trusted me to keep my word.

But then she called. And called. And called again. Even with my Society mask on, she knew it was me taking all her orders.

She asked me my name and *I gave it to her*. I broke one of the few rules I have as a courier and I gave her my name.

I'm not supposed to get attached.

She's not supposed to know my name or identity, yet she wouldn't stop.

She followed me. Stalked me like one of her prey. And I let her. I couldn't stop her. I didn't want to.

She's not just Pandora from the myth, she's the box too. Once she's opened, there's no stopping the flood that follows the demise.

Even after her box has opened, I can't help the hope that she leaves in me.

She chose me, chose me and Eros to be obsessed with. I caught the eye of the most beautiful woman I know. How fucking lucky am I?

I'll make her shine again. I'd do anything for her, including helping her find herself. No matter the cost. Even if it'll cause her to hate me in the end.

I'd do it. For her. Always for her. Always for him.

Then the Mafia stepped on the scene and she got scared. Truly scared. Not for herself, but for her Dad. For me.

This was different from the time in the warehouse. That time we were a team, with excitement lacing our blood. Now this was a rescue mission. One I hope we've made it on time for.

I don't know if Pandora could take losing her Dad, not like this. I have to do everything in my power to save him.

"We kill Marcel and Bruno, then we'll let Pandora get the rest if she so pleases." Eros confirms the plan as we get to Bruno Yearwood's house in Detroit. It's more a mansion, bigger than Marcel's, and off the bat we can tell these men play more pissing games than actual work.

He's got bodyguards at the front of his walkway, then two more at his front door. He's got another set flanking each side of his house too and that lets me know Bruno's paranoid. Someone really is after him.

I could find who and why, if I cared. But I don't. I only care about Pandora's freedom. Mine was never in jeopardy, but in her eyes it was, so I guess mine, too.

Eros follows behind me as I approach the guards on the side. This time around, I made sure the cameras were off so the guards inside wouldn't catch us.

They all are responsible for hurting Pandora and, for that, I have no qualms about killing every single one of them.

Approaching the first guy within my reach, I stab a knife through the guy's neck and slowly drop him to the ground. Eros does the same for someone else. All I can hear is the grunt of a kill, and I'm moving inside.

Moving to the front of the door, my hand rests on the handle and finds it's unlocked. I nod at Eros, who nods back, pulling his gun out. I grab mine with one hand and swing open the door with the other. The guards on the inside freeze at our entrance and I take that as my moment to shoot.

Three bodies drop before they register what's going on. Eros shoves me to the right as he jumps toward the left. I take cover behind a side table at the entry way as Eros dives behind a piano.

Bullets whip past us. Bruno's main entry has those two stair sets that go upstairs and there are about four guys shooting at us.

"Go," Eros yells and I pop up from my cover. In the video it appeared as if Pandora's Dad was in a basement, so we have minutes to get there and hopefully Bruno doesn't call any more fucking guards.

We dart towards the remaining guards. All I hear are bullets, screams, and grunts.

It's not something I'm used to, but I'm grateful for it. I don't want to focus on the kill cause I'm not a killer. I'm not. I protect what is mine. Eros and Pandora, and by extension Pandora's Dad, are mine to protect.

They are my family.

Mine.

"Let's find Pandora's Dad," Eros says. He's out of breath with blood splattered over his tan skin. I wordlessly reach a hand up to wipe it and he lets me. I take this moment to make sure he's okay.

"How many rounds do you have left?" Eros asks to take my gun and check. His gaze moves back to me and shakes his head. None.

"You?" I ask. I slide my knife back out from earlier and fist it in my hands. He nods his head no. We are down to knives in a gunfight.

I sigh. Let's fucking do this. We rush back down the stairs and open every fucking door on our way through the house, looking for the basement. Now that the guards are dead, the house is eerily quiet and I can't tell if it sets my nerves alive or is the reason for the pit in my stomach.

Pandora's Dad may already be dead if it's quiet.

My hand rests on the door right beside the kitchen. I have a gut instinct. This is the right door and I look up at Eros.

"Ready," he whispers and I yank open the door. The first guard must have heard us coming as he was right on the other side of the door, but clearly wasn't ready for us to be here. He fumbles for his gun, but Eros is quick to stab him, his gun dropping to the ground as his hands reach his neck. Eros grabs his gun and takes out the two guards at the bottom, who are truly too slow to be considered guards whatsoever. The Society would have a field day with this bunch.

We race down the creaky stairs to find Bruno and Marcel. Bruno stands from his chair at a table off to the side and Marcel stands over Pandora's Dad. Seeing the camera and tripod ignites a flame in my gut that spreads all throughout my body. It must for Eros cause he's on Marcel before I can fucking blink. Eros empties the gun and discards the bullets before plummeting into Marcel.

My gaze moves to Bruno, who moves to pull his gun on Eros. I lunge toward him, knocking the gun out of his hand and punching him. I could have used my knife, but I'm not here to kill Bruno. No. I'm here to get him ready for the person who deserves to take his last breath.

His foot slams down on my leg and I land on one knee as he punches across my face. My head snaps, but I grab his leg and yank. Pulling him down to the ground. Ignoring the burning pain in my cheek and I move over him and land blow after blow over his face. I watch the blood spurt from his mouth and drip from his nose, and I can't stop. I feel him try to jerk to get some sort of advantage, but Bruno isn't the man he used to be.

He's gotten lazy hiding behind guards since his reign.

His skin rips under my knuckles and I love the way that feels. The control I have over his life runs a small thrill over my skin. I won't kill him, I can't. Not yet. Not until Pandora gets here.

This beef is between him and her.

I stop, my chest heaving as I stare at Bruno.

"Please," His pathetic whimpers irritate me. Bruno Yearwood, the Don of the Detroit Mafia, should've been harder to get to. Harder to fight and here he is whispering and fucking crying.

"Shut the fuck up," I mutter, standing and grabbing him by his neck and lifting him up, too.

A door slamming open grabs my attention. Pandora comes flying in, her hair and eyes wild as she scans over the room.

It's time to finish this. It's time for her to be free.

Chapter 17

Pandora

The basement door blows open as I slam my shoulder into it. I find Eros and Kohen as they fight, but my eyes don't stop till I see the person I came here for. Scanning over the room, my eyes are like magnets and I see my Dad. Stock is still on the floor and my heart fucking cracks.

I think it cracks; it hurts like it cracked. I grip my chest as my legs carry me to my Dad. He's on the floor facing away from me and I sob as I pull on his shoulder to face me.

His face is ashen, like a gray layer has been painted underneath his skin. His cheeks are wet with blood and tears, and I can hardly look at him. How could I have let this happen?

"Daddy," I whisper as his eyes meet mine. He blinks. I let out a breath of relief as I sob over him. He moves so his hand pats my back, but by the grimace on his face, I think the action is too much for him.

"You have to run, little one, please," my dad whispers. He tries to lean up, but he can't. Trying to push me away, he repeats his words as I cling onto him.

"Never," I promise. "I'm so sorry, Dad. This is all my fault." I sob against his chest and he shakes his head, but he doesn't understand.

He doesn't understand I could've solved all our problems if I hadn't got scared.

"It's okay, I'll fix this Dad, I swear." I get him to lean up against a wall as he tries to plead for me to run, but I came prepared this time. I'm ready.

Turning around, I spot Eros, who has Marcel pinned down on the ground with his knee digging into his back and a gun pressed against his forehead.

Kohen has Bruno, a man I hardly know, yet is the cause of all my problems, confined in a chokehold and a gun pressed against his ribs.

Tears streams down my face but all that pain faded to the back of my brain as I stare between the two men in front of me. As much as I want to torture the both of them, there is no time.

I have to get my Dad to a hospital.

Taking the gun Eros let me borrow a while ago, I grasp it in my hands. Feeling the weight of the gun and the weight of the lives in this room. It's all up to me now. I'm the one in control. I'm the one in charge.

I'm the one with a gun to their heads this time.

As much as I'd love to take them both back to my studio to torture them until they die. I don't have that kind of time. My dad doesn't have that kind of time. Bringing the gun up, both hands gripping the gun. I turn to Bruno first. "I hope your rule was fun because it's over now."

"My hell becomes yours honey, good luck with Bear." He has the gull to smile at me with his dark brown eyes. I can see the weight of his greed in them. I see in his smile he regrets nothing. Nothing up until this point, and that's when I know I've found someone truly evil.

Someone like me.

Death isn't scary. Not when you have nothing to lose. Bruno never had anything to lose, which means he's already lost his rule of the Mafia.

It might have been gone before we even got here.

This "Bear" is probably on his way here. Bruno would rather us kill him than whatever is after him and for a moment I hesitate. The last thing any of us need is an encounter with whom he calls "Bear."

I steady the heavy gun in my head. My lessons from the shooting range sparking my trigger finger. The hot metal jolts me back as I shoot Bruno between the eyes.

He goes slack in Kohen's arms. The impact forces Kohen to jagger back. He drops Bruno's body. His warm gray-brown eyes comfort me. I'm close to running into his arms, seeking that warmth out, but the night isn't over.

"I don't remember a Bear?" Kohen mumbles, but I don't have time to digest. I barely have time to fucking think. All that's on my mind now is getting my Dad help before that fucker appears.

"Please, Pandora, you don't have to do this. You got your lick back, you have the Mafia–" I shot him in the shoulder.

"Your begging isn't as sweet as I imagined," I say. Rolling my lips, I sigh in disappointment. I wanted to see him cry, beg, piss himself. Hell, I wanted to make him bleed to death. A slow, painful death lasting over days and I can't. I never will.

This will have to be enough.

"Marcel, you took advantage of me," I say as I squat down in front of him. Eros still has him trapped in his arms as he yanks Marcel's head up to face me. His brown hair is slick with sweat and dirt. His skin is wet under his tears and, for once, Marcel isn't the biggest guy in the room. He isn't the strongest, he isn't anything.

Marcel Amos is nothing.

"But I never forced to have sex, I wasn't going too, I–" He cries. I tisk, shaking my head as I trace the head of the gun along his face.

"No, but let's not pretend it wasn't headed there. Tell me Marcel, honestly, was my Dad ever safe?"

He doesn't answer. He stares at me. We sit in silence for a moment. I don't think my Dad can afford. My eyes glance over at him.

My Dad lies still on the floor, unable to move, but I see his chest move up and down, showing he's breathing. I don't know how much time I have left.

My Dad means more than revenge to me. Still, it stings knowing I have to wrap this up early.

It stings knowing my Dad is here to hear this. To hear his daughter kill his villains. Still, I'm running out of time. I can feel the itch up my arms. My Dad is dying.

Snapping my gaze back to Marcel, I pry his mouth open with the head of the gun and I smile. I may not have a lot of time but I can enjoy this moment. This rush of power. Marcel Amos's life is mine and nothing can take that away from me.

Not even time.

Marcel's slobber coats the gun and some lands on the floor. His body violently shakes as he pleads with his eyes. *No, please don't. I'll do anything. Don't shoot.* I wish I could hear the words coming from him, but the mental voice in my head will have to suffice.

Eros keeps Marcel's head forward so he can't slide off the gun. I hold my breath as I meet Eros's eyes. He keeps my gaze, his brown eyes meeting my own. A bruise is forming around his right eye. It'll probably be black in the morning. He doesn't say anything, only nods his head a single time. I take that as all confirmation I need and meet Marcel's stare again.

"We both know the answer, don't we, and that is your true crime Marcel," I say, pull the trigger.

Blood splatters all over my face as the shot sounds in the room. The eerily silence of the room is oddly comforting.

"It's done," I whisper as Kohen's arms wrap from behind me. His strong arms hold my middle, hold me together as Eros drops Marcel's body and pulls me into his arms. We move as one fluid motion as I fall into them. Holy fuck.

I *killed* the Mafia heads. Eros and Kohen killed pretty much everyone else.

Swallowing my sobs, I look over to my dad, whose eyes are closed now, but I see his chest fall and raise.

The night is not fucking over.

"Let's go," Eros says, letting go of me and picking my Dad up, wrapping one arm under him as he gets him to stand. My Dad's feet dangle as Kohen swoops in on the other side and helps carry him.

"Princess, get the doors for us please," Eros's voice breaks me from the trance as I rush over to the door, holding it open for them.

I barely see the dead bodies littered everywhere as we rush to the car. Kohen gets my Dad in the car and sits in the back with him as Eros guides me to the front.

"I need to be by him," I say as he pulls my seatbelt over my chest.

"Let Ko tend to the wounds that he can," Eros says as he shuts my door and runs over to the diver's side.

"He's breathing, a few bruises and cuts on his skin, can't tell of anything deeper and nothing explains his lack of mobility," Kohen reports. I watch him through the rearview mirror as he tends to my Dad, putting cream and ice packs over his skin. He pries his eyes open and the white of my Dad's eyes scares me as Kohen flashes a light.

"Is he okay?"

"He'll live," Eros says, stepping on the gas. Breaking all sorts of laws as we get to the Litchfort hospital.

"Please help him," I murmur even as I watch Kohen do his best to help him. I render useless as I watch him work. Restlessness fills my arms like the urge to stretch. I almost reach out to them, but I can't risk getting in the way. "Dad, it's gonna be okay, I swear."

He doesn't respond and my heart drops so hard I whip around to face the window, unable to look any more.

He's okay. He's okay. He has to be okay.

"We're here." Eros's words snap me into action as I fly out the car and whip open the backseat door. Eros runs off and all I can focus on is my Dad. The hospital has a round driveway probably reserved for ambulances, but Eros didn't care. We are parked here and the nurses rush out behind Eros with a gurney. Three of them come to help and I move out of the way to let them get my Dad.

I back into Eros's chest as his hands rest on my shoulders, rubbing them as Kohen slides out of the car.

"I'll park, follow them," Kohen says, hopping into the driver's seat and pulling off.

"Let's go Princess," Eros says, pulling my hand as we race after the nurses and my Dad. We only make it so far before they stop us.

"Sit here, don't move," Eros says as he guides me down into one of the chairs. I bring my hands up to my face, cupping my cheeks as I reel in as to what happened tonight. I killed Marcel Amos and Bruno Yearwood.

My Dad is hurt, I know he is. If he lives through whatever happened before I got there, his life will be altered forever. I've seen someone's legs look so stiff yet loose. So unmoveable. It's not a weight I wish to see on my dad, on Eros, on Kohen.

"Hey," Kohen says, kneeling in front of me. When did he get here? I gulp as my eyes meet his. "He'll be okay. The nurses and doctors will take care of him here."

I exhale as he speaks in his soothing voice, trying to process his words as truth. As reality.

I nod and he brings his hands up to my face, probably wiping blood off, or maybe smudging it in. I don't care. I lean into his hand and he takes his hands away from my face only to swoop me into his arms, sitting with me in his lap. Patting my hair as he whispers affirmations that my dad will be okay and that we can handle this.

My heart slows as he rocks me gently, as much as he possibly can in these hospital chairs. Soon I see Eros come towards us with a clipboard in his hands. I go to reach for it, but he swats my hand away.

"I got it," he says.

"How? He's *my* Dad?" I ask, scrunching my brows.

"When I say I know everything about you, that includes your Dad," He murmurs as he fills out the paperwork.

"Oh," I say. I lean back into Kohen. Trying to catch his calming scent of musk and laundry detergent, but it's nowhere to be found. Fuck.

"We need showers," I mutter, knowing we aren't going to do anything about it. I'm not leaving my dad, and they aren't leaving me.

"That's too bad," Eros says, not even looking at me. I guess it's better he fills out the paperwork.

I wonder if we scare anyone here being covered in blood. Is it normal here? Maybe I should've been a doctor or a nurse... Nah, too many hours and too much fucking school.

Oh my God, school... university, I just killed my scholarship, literally.

But I got my Dad and we're free. Just as long as no one steps up to be a Mafia Don. I sigh, trying to curl into Kohen. How long will that be? What happens when another Bruno comes in and takes over our debt?

"Stop thinking," Kohen whispers against my forehead.

"What are you thinking about?" I ask. He sighs as he looks away from me. I watch him as he thinks.

"I'm thinking about you," He says. "I'm thinking about how I should've watched your Dad closer, should've killed Bruno and Marcel before they had the chance to hurt you."

"Nothing you could've done would've changed this outcome. This was on me."

"No, not on you. This was on Bruno and Marcel." He says it like he truly believes it. We both know if I wouldn't have tried to go on my path of vengeance, this probably wouldn't have happened.

Vengeance isn't always the answer, even when you kill people for sport.

I should've killed them, taken what I wanted, their lives, from the start. But I didn't and now my Dad has to pay the price of that. Of not only my fear, but my revenge.

"Family of Dan Melrose."

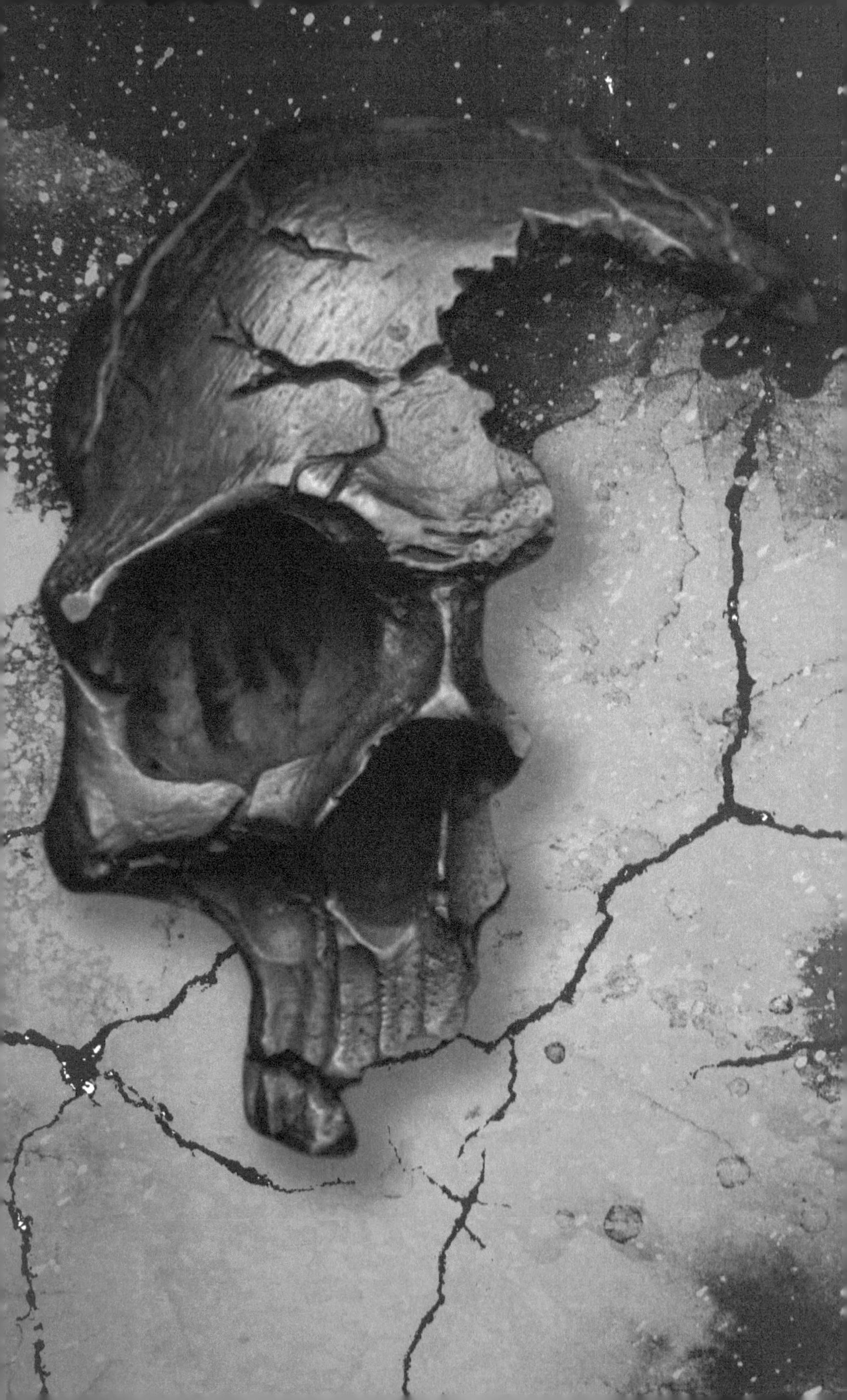

Chapter 18

Kohen

"We are super close, Mr. Melrose," I say as I help, well, carry Pandora's Dad up the stairs to his porch and into the house.

Dan Melrose survived the attack, but he lost all mobility in the lower half of his body. He no longer has control over his legs and feet. He can't work or move on his own. At least not until he adjusts to his new life.

Pandora's sobs in that hospital room still ring in my ears. I can still feel her sobs racking through her body under my hand. The news appeared to hurt Pandora more than it did her Dad.

She blames herself. She's the only one who blames herself. The Mafia was always coming after her Dad. His debt was his, and taking his daughter was only a punishment to him. Never to her.

"You are such a sweet young man, please, just help me towards the couch," He says. His voice is weathered, and he's trying his best to be polite. Kind. It amazes me. How someone who has gone through the things he has remains positive.

I only hum in response as I set him down on the couch. Pandora and Eros are getting his bags from the car.

After getting him settled, I go to help them out, but Mr. Melrose grabs my arm.

"Wait, son, tell me. Who are you to, my daughter? I know you ain't no nurse," He asks.

I chuckle, feeling my cheeks flame. "Yeah, I guess it's time to address that huh?" I ask, moving to take a seat in one of the armchairs across from him.

The Melroses has a comfortable living room. Warm-colored furniture with a small tv that is collecting a thin layer of dust on it.

"I'm... well, I'm courting Pandora." The words sound good coming from my lips. I can't stop the smile that takes over my face.

"And what about that other boy?"

"So is he."

"So you're competing."

"Not quite." I say.

"Oh," He chuckles and despite his chuckle, I can see the shock on his face. Both his eyebrows are raised as he turns his head to stare at his daughter, who walks in.

"My Little one isn't so little anymore, huh," He says as he tackles her hand in his.

"What?" she says, confused, and I offer a half shrug. I'll let them have that conversation.

"Ahh, nothing," Mr. Melrose says as he turns back to me. "What's for dinner, nurse?"

I laugh as I stare at Pandora and Eros. They settle Mr. Melrose's things down as they look around the place.

This house isn't made for people with Mr. Melrose's disability. The steep stairs and closed concept isn't helpful in the slightest.

"We could have takeout?"

"We've had takeout for the last few weeks, put that cooking class to work," Mr. Melrose says with a deep laugh. His head falls back as if the joke was that funny.

"To work?" Eros says with raised eyebrows.

"Yeah, tough guy put those classes to work," Pandora says, dragging him to the kitchen. I chuckle, following behind them.

This is what I wanted. Them, a house, a real family. I can feel the sense of belonging when I'm around the Melroses. It's exactly what I imagined being part of a family would feel like.

A place, a group of people I can breathe around without thinking. A place I can just *be*.

"What are we making, boys?" Pandora says, clasping her hands together as she leans against the counter. Her sweats hang low off her hips and the pink matching jacket is short enough to show the soft skin of her waist. She slings an apron with frills on, handing me a matching one and throwing one at Eros.

I laugh as he catches it. Holding it out with scrunched brows. "Why do you have three?"

"I knew I'd have people here to wear them with me one day." She shrugs. I smile to myself. Pandora always knew we'd be here some day. I wish I wouldn't have taken so long to come to the same conclusion.

"We hardly have been to class, let alone enough to know what to cook," Eros chuckles, tying the pink ruffle apron around his waist.

"What does your Dad like?" I ask. I open her fridge to find ingredients to make something.

"Tacos?" she says, dipping under my arm and stepping in front of me. She pulls out taco fixings and I slide out of her way. Eros finds a pot after opening nearly every cabinet, even though they were next to the stove, and I drop the meat in.

"Someone's here," Mr. Melrose yells from his chair. I wash my hands and Eros goes to answer the door with Pandora on his heels. I think it is all good when I hear the door shut, but no footsteps of Pandora and Eros coming back. I scrunch my brows and dry my hands before walking to the front door. I see Mr. Melrose on the couch with his phone in his hands and a video playing on the front porch. I feel for the gun in my waistband.

Just in case.

I open the front door and Pandora instantly reaches out for me. Her hand wraps around my bicep and I close the door. There's a man here. He stands with his arms crossed and dressed in all black. He's a black man with deep dark skin and short hair like mine.

"What's going on?" I ask, curling an arm around Pandora and standing next to Eros.

"You won't fucking believe who this is." Eros says.

"Bear." Pandora fills in, quickly scrunching her eyebrows.

"Bear?" I ask, the name rattling in my head. Bruno mentioned dealing with a Bear, but... what is he doing here?

"Bear." The man confirms, with a nod of his head. "I'm here cause I found Bruno and Marcel's dead bodies."

"So what now?" Eros asks, flexing his arms. He's ready to pounce and I should, too.

"I figured I'd pay their killers a visit..." He stops and watches our faces. His eyes are the darkest I've ever seen. So dark the whites of them appear to shine. He's careful yet confident and regardless of his intentions, I'm ready for whatever he has planned.

"Find a point and get to it, please," Pandora says, her face a mask of confusion.

"I'm taking the head of the Mafia. I'm letting you know. You have fair claim to it–"

"Don't want it." Eros cuts in, shaking his head.

"Don't change your mind, I'm not an easy kill," He chuckles and I nearly crack a smile myself.

"Neither are we," I say, cocking my head.

"Consider your family's debt paid then, Pandora. The Mafia mine to fix now, starting with your family."

"Starting with?" Pandora asks, curiosity seeking in.

"From now on, we don't ruin people who are only looking to better their situation. Not if we can help it," Bear says with a shrug, as if this change was obvious. Maybe it was to him, a Mafia man, and maybe it should have been to me, a Society man.

I see a plan, a calculated plan in his eyes, and this may have been the first time I've felt comfortable with someone. Something about his aura is threatening, but in a way I'm familiar with.

Bear could've been a Society man. He could just be a man from Detroit. Either way, a man with a code is a man I don't have to worry about.

"I don't want anything to do with the Mafia, forget about the Melrose's, and we won't come after you," Pandora says, still safely tucked between Eros and I.

"I think I know when not to tempt stone cold killers," Bear laughs. Leaving us with one final nod, he walks off the porch towards a Porsche. We watch him drive off and for once, everything feels... right.

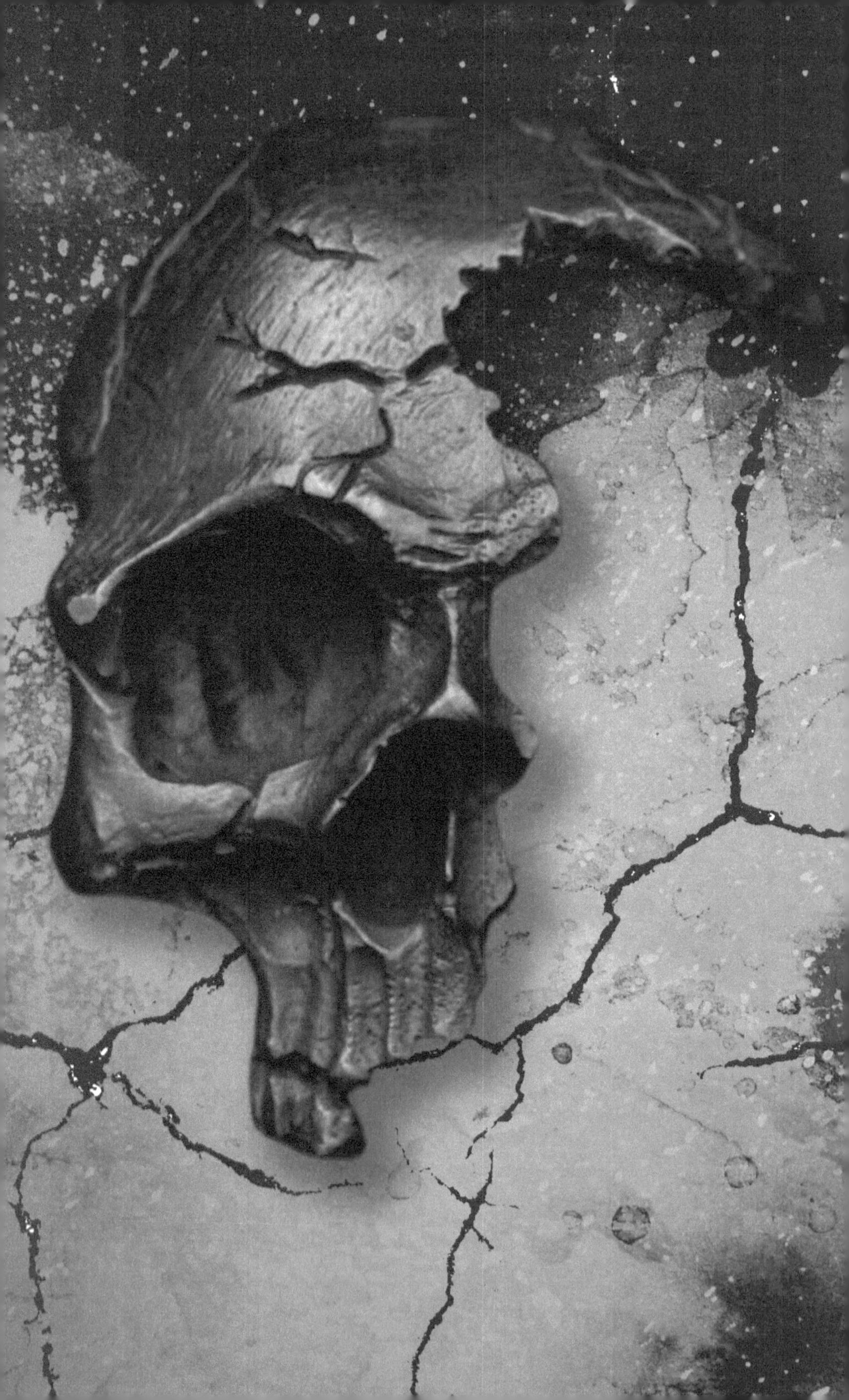

Chapter 19

Pandora

Becoming my Dad's caretaker–eh, trying to be my Dad's caretaker has been a journey and after getting him into bed, I decided to take some time to myself.

My art studio has been missing me since... since the incident and the itch to paint is stronger than any night thus far. Now that we are settling into our new routine, I'm more than ready to get back into painting. More so killing.

A body is locked in the chains coming from the ceiling. This time it's Samuel, my ex-classmate, and the last remaining Mafia member who stood by Marcel and Bruno, hangs there. He told my new friend, Juliet, her business idea of selling soaps was stupid and that was truly my last straw.

I don't kill off a whim, though there are moments I've thought about it. I'm not a good person by any means and don't view myself as a vigilante but, still, I like purpose.

I can't look my Dad in the eye without purpose. Not that he knows his daughter is a murderer. He doesn't remember how Marcel and Bruno died. He's never been a *questions* kind of guy.

Sighing, I go back to my canvas. I'm trying something different this time. I'm jumping out of my comfort zone. Instead of landscapes or forest animals, I have a box in the middle of my canvas. A black open box, antique style with matter coming out of it. I think the matter should be red.

Turning, I clasp my hands on my knees as Samuel tries to lift himself to loosen the pressure of the chains.

I shed my cable-knit sweater; it is one of my favorites. My outfit tonight is for a special call, an homage to normalcy. Kohen and Eros are on their way, which means I have fifteen mines to get Samuel where I want him.

My perfect little gift.

"What the fuck is going on?" Samuel shouts as if he hasn't asked only about a million fucking times already. I sigh as he spits, or tries to, at me, but I'm too far away.

My outfit is too cute for that.

A brown dress almost too short to cover my ass is all I had underneath the sweater. It's all I needed for my sweet man, Kohen, and my asshole, Eros, to get here.

Hearing their sharp knock, I rush to the door, giggles escaping my lips as Samuel screams for help.

"Hey boys," I say, leaning against the doorframe. Eros holds a pizza box in his hands, and Kohen smiles at me as he dives for me. Strong arms wrap around my waist as I'm lifted into the air. His lips attack mine as he walks us inside. I grab his face as I kiss him, his soft skin under my hands as his scent engulfs me.

I smile into his kiss as he steps me on my feet. I press a light kiss to his nose as I'm pulled away into Eros's arms, who snuggles his nose into the crook of my neck.

"Hey to you too Princess," He says as he takes a deep inhale and then pulls away.

"Don't pretend like you don't fucking see me," Samuel, my gift, yells wiggling from his chain in the ceiling.

"You saw my request," I say, opening the pizza box on my desk.

"You used the Society's services to deliver a pizza. Can't say I've done that before," Kohen says as he sits on one of my stools around the room. I smile.

"I had to get you here," I say, loading three plates with pizza.

"A call or text wouldn't have sufficed?" Eros says, eating his pizza.

"Not while you're on the clock, no," I say. "Not for what I have planned."

"And what is that?" Eros asks.

"Dinner and show." And a fuck if I'm lucky.

Kohen's eyes meet mine and I swear they look darker. As if the gray in them has vanished for something more sinister.

"A fucking show? Look, I'm sorry, I'm so fucking sorry," Samuel's incessantly annoying mouthing is ruining the moment. Rolling my eyes, I take a dagger from one of my drawers.

I slowly walk towards Samuel, his demands becoming whiny cries as I twist the dagger between my fingers. The sharp end cuts my fingertips, but what's fun without a little pain? A little blood?

Or a lot of blood, in Samuel's case.

I cackle as his piss slides down his legs and lands on the floor. I hear the guys snicker behind me, but I stop once I realize I have to clean that up.

Fuck.

"You see this painting," I say. Samuel doesn't answer, only cries. Which I guess is fair? He is about to die and maybe it's settling in. "It's missing something."

"What's missing, baby?" Kohen asks.

"Red," I say. I gaze at Eros, who sets down his pizza, and comes to me. "I want his tongue."

"You can't do it?" He asks, amusement in his eyes.

"I'm not tall enough," I playfully pout. I grab one of my paint bowls and hold it underneath his mouth, ready to catch my new paint. "Kohen, can you hold his feet?"

He moves silently and as he gets closer, I watch his face. Kohen is my sweetman. Meaning he's sweet, kind, gentle even, but you don't get into this business being sweet, kind or gentle. Kohen has a monster in him like the rest of us. He doesn't need to come out and play as often as Eros or mine does.

I protect Kohen's monster as he protects me. He's not used to it yet, but in time he will be and it will all be thanks to me.

You're welcome, baby.

Kohen bends down and his hands wrap around Samuel's weak ankles like bands of steel. This shit is gonna hurt. Maybe next time he won't say some dumb shit that'll make a killer like me target him. No one makes fun of my friends' ideas, no matter how new of a friend the friend may be.

"I'd told you I'd kill you," Eros says as Samuel begs and pleads with him. Eros shrugs as he makes go for his tongue. His screams die as Eros leans his head back and slices off his tongue. Because the dagger isn't the sharpest, he has to saw at it a few times, but that gives me all the blood I need.

"How the hell are we going to eat pizza covered in blood?" Eros as he tosses the tongue aside. I tilt my head in thought. Shit, I hadn't thought of that.

"Oops," I say as I skip back to my painting.

"You guys are done. I got what I needed." I straddle my stool, the cool metal stinging my bare thighs as I sit. "There's a sink over there to wash off."

I don't bother washing off as I stare down at the ruby red blood in my bowl. It doesn't swish like water. In fact, his blood is quite thick and healthy.

"Open," Kohen says and I turn to face him. He stands beside me with a slice of pizza and I softly smile.

I take a bite of the pizza slice in his hands and I almost melt at how cute he is. How his eyes light up as she feeds me while I paint with Samuel's blood.

I replaced what was going to be black matter with red, mixing the blood with red paint so it'll stick to the canvas. I paint my little pandora's box. Cracked open and spilled all the badness into the surrounding space.

Grabbing some white, I add highlights to the box so it appears as if it lights up from the inside. I was Pandora, the woman who opened the box. I let the worst come out before fighting my fear and taking what I wanted. I let it all out before I could shut the box again.

I watch as Eros and Kohen converse, but their words don't register in my head. As I stare at them, I can't help the warmth that comes over me like a shower.

Now I have what's left. The hope.

I love them and I get to keep them.

How nice.

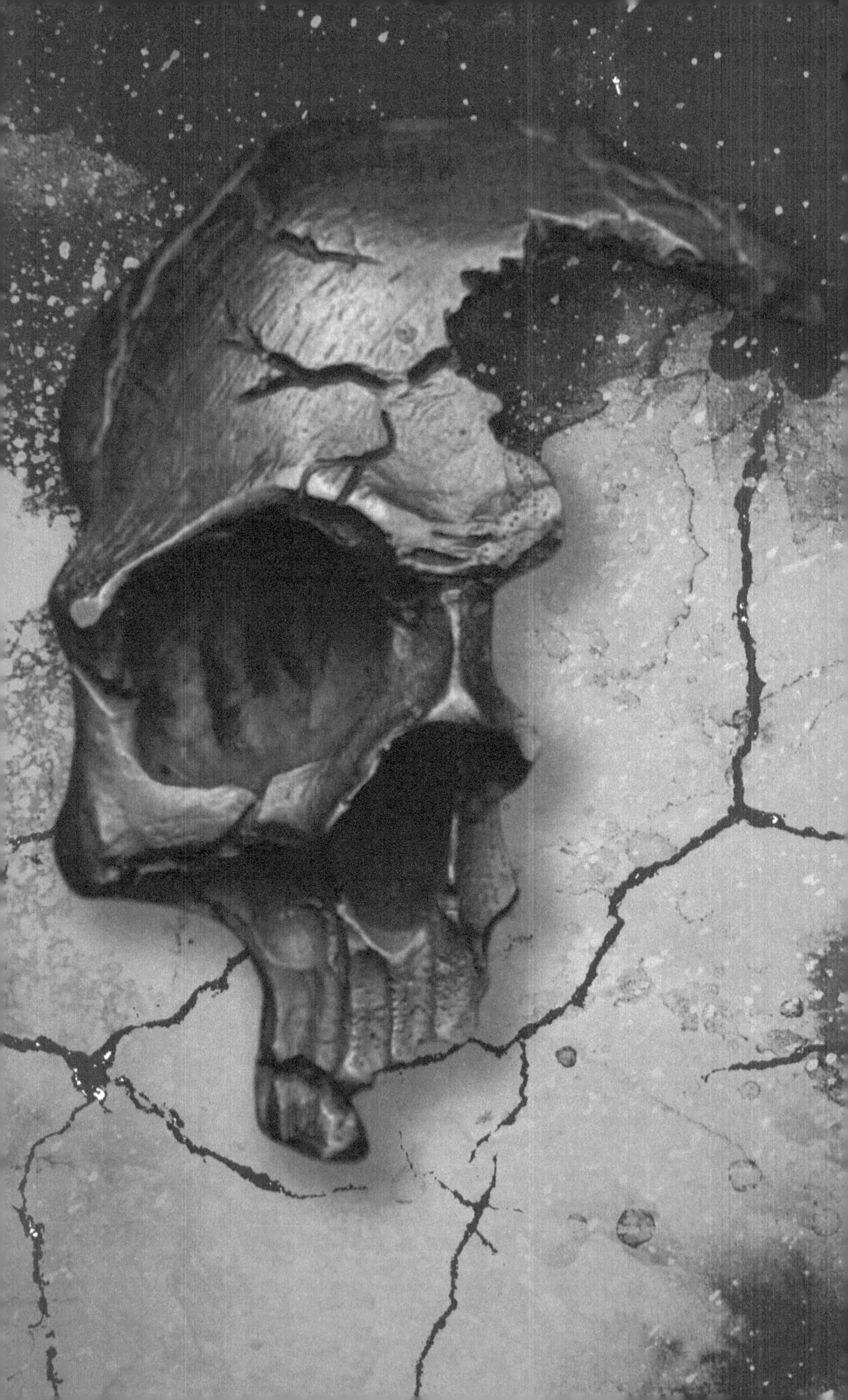

Epilogue

Eros

Being our last job, Kohen and I accepted the request to work the annual ball in Paris for the Society. While it would have been more fun to attend, we admittedly aren't on the same level as these folks, or even as Pandora.

We're not killers in the same way, though, Kohen could probably get there with Pandora's influence. I strictly kill to protect. If there is nothing to protect, then I don't kill.

But my sweet, loving Princess Pandora is different. Upon finding out we were working, what does Pandora Melrose do?

She ensures she makes the eight kills required so that she can go too. Discounting anything she did earlier in the year. She made eight kills in the span of a week all by herself. Let's say, that week she was extremely busy and it was the longest week of our lives, but hey, we're all going to Paris.

The flight here was more than fun, since I rented out a private plane. I fucked both my partners the whole way here and I couldn't wait for the flight back home.

We had to leave Pandora unescorted for tonight, since we worked the Friday introduction and dinner. Thankfully, we didn't have to work the whole ball, though, we can't attend it at all unless we come as Pandora's plus one, which she only asked Kohen, that fucking little brat.

She won't tell me what her plans are either and the jobs are booked up for the weekend, so I'll be in Paris alone.

"Think she'll behave tonight?" Kohen says with a waitstaff uniform on. My job is obvious. I stand guard at the entrance most of the night in a black suit, then stand over the dinner to ensure no one tries anything. Pretty simple.

Couriers run around like chickens with their heads cut off, escorting members wherever they need to be, cutting surveillance of the airport cameras so members aren't seen. It's a fuck ton of work to ensure authorities don't find out a bunch of serial killers are meeting all at the same spot at one time.

What a fucking field day they'd have.

"Pandora? In Paris? Hell no, she won't behave. If anything, this will be our hardest working weekend," I chuckle as Kohen shakes his head with a smile on his lips. We haven't seen her since we had to leave at the ass crack of dawn, but knowing her, she's got Paris all figured out and if she doesn't... Well then there will be a line of dead bodies following her.

Tonight is a special night that many wait for all year. Tonight's Host is Elliot Jay, he's from Litchfort, Michigan too. He and his girlfriend have had a few deliveries Kohen and I had handled. They're pretty clean though, since they appreciate the "art" of a kill. From the hunt to clean up, they say.

Many guests dressed in this year's theme, black, gold, and silver and wearing masks, walk up to the black carpet of this year's venue, the Musée de la Chasse et de la Nature. Kohen and I work on scanning everyone's rings as they come in, verifying they actually got an invitation.

I mindlessly get into a groove. The minutes tick by as I wordlessly scan each member in. I don't have to say anything as most of these members have been a part of the Society for years. They know the drill as much as I do and if they don't, they figure it out faster than I can put into words.

Hours pass, and I start to think Pandora isn't coming. I watch the sun start to set and the stars start to appear in the sky. Kohen has made his rounds from helping out here, to back inside, and now he's here with me waiting for our Princess to arrive.

Then I see her.

I see my Princess dressed like a princess walking towards me. The event is black tie, but she dressed like royalty. When did she even have time to get that dress? She strides forward in a black ball gown dress. The top is the tightest corset type top I've ever seen and it's got black crystals hanging off it like teardrops and black pearls on strings dangling from the top. It's got so many details, so many layers.

It's perfect for her.

The dress drags on the floor with a slit too high for most. The skirt moves like thick waves around her, as if they move to please her and fuck. She's the most beautiful woman I've ever seen.

"You could drop dead at my beauty while you're at it. It'd really stroke my ego," she says as she pretends to flip her hair, but that's in a fancy type bun.

"You look gorgeous, baby," Kohen says in the same awe I'm experiencing. He takes her delicate hand, her nails long and painted black, and presses a kiss on the back of her hand before scanning in her ring.

I hear a cough and I'm brought away from Pandora to scan in another member. I quickly scan them, if not only to see Pandora wink at me as she glides past us. My eyes find Kohen's and he's grinning like a damn cat.

"I'm so taking off that dress tonight," he mutters.

"Not if I take it off first," I snicker. Since she invited him as her plus one to this weekend's ball, the least she could do was let me take her dress off.

Glancing at my watch, it's close to time for the dinner and I nod to Kohen. The last of the members who will get in tonight get scanned in and I make my way to the dining hall. This is quite the museum. It's beautiful with all the decor and it's unique to see all the vendors selling things in the halls and the workshops for the weekend getting set up. The Society truly goes all out for these balls.

Kohen goes to the kitchen. His duties change to being a server for the rest of the night, while I get to stand here and look pretty. Standing inside the dining hall, I watch as members converse before finding their tables and taking a seat. It's rare anyone acts out of turn here, as the Society is quick to pull the trigger and has the means to hide dead bodies as silently as the dead of night.

These nights are truly meant for fun.

Elliot Jay, the host, stands and makes his way towards the stage. He's blond, but not the cherry kind. I've never seen him smile. He takes care of everything he does with the utmost care and precision. He doesn't trust a soul besides the one he calls Brother, and his weapon of choice is a wire saw. That shit gets messy as hell and is not fun to clean up afterwards at all.

I helped him one time, one time he called for body bags and I offered to help. Never did I ever make that mistake again.

Kohen laughed every time I gagged. But hell, what is one's reaction supposed to be when picking up someone's head? Only their head, no body attached. The fucker sawed it off.

"Welcome to Mortes Ostium's annual ball," Elliot begins his speech, but my eyes are glued to Pandora. She sits amongst other killers, like herself. She talks and laughs and even though I can't hear her, I smile.

I love watching her as much as I love being with her. I am a Guard at the end of the day. I've been trained my whole life to be a Guard and today's my last day.

Today's my *last* day.

"Hey lover boy," I hear one of my fellow guards whisper. I turn to look at him. I raise my eyebrows, wondering why the fuck he interrupted my gazing.

As if there was something more important than my time watching my Princess.

"You're needed down in the kitchen."

"By who?"

"Since when the fuck do I look like I ask questions?" He says with a laugh and I shake my head.

"Since day one, fucker," I mutter as I pass him, leaving my post to go to the kitchen. Did a higher up need me? One of our leaders, maybe?

I stride to the kitchen, running a hand through my hair, wondering what the hell is going on.

My arm is tugged and suddenly I'm in a kitchen, or at least a kitchen much smaller than the main with a deviously looking Pandora and Kohen staring at me.

"I have to report," I say, but Pandora cuts me off with a tisk wagging her slim finger.

"You have to report to me," Pandora says. The glint of mischief in her eyes tells me she set me up to this and Kohen is the one that told her how. Heat rushes up my cheeks and still I smirk at the two disasters in front of me. I love these two and the headaches they cause me. The looks on both faces make everything worth it. Absolutely everything.

Pandora yanks me by my neck and kisses me like she owns me. Like this is the first kiss of many over the span of a lifetime. Her lips are soft against mine and her hands rake in my hair and down my neck and shoulders.

I let out a moan between our lips and she stops with a sly smile. Holding my gaze, she floats down. Kneeling in front of me, her dress poofs out around her like a true princess. Kohen squats beside her, his hand possessively grabbing her neck.

Her hands reach the waistband of my pants and I'm tugged forward.

"I've yet to get a taste of you, and I'm craving a lick," she says. Her voice dripping in a desperation building in my gut.

Her fingers pull my dress shirt from my pants. Light touches dance across my skin and I nearly buckle from want.

"Don't play with your food, Pandora," I mutter, trying to keep my hips from chasing her fingers. She giggles, the lightest I've heard her voice in far too long as she stares at me. Grasping the zipper of my pants, she slowly unzips me, my bulge painfully pressing against my pants, finding the tiniest bit of relief. Fuck. I stare at my Princess and my Prince holding her.

"Aww, my poor baby needs some attention?" Pandora asks, moving her gaze to my bulge. I nod but she doesn't respond, keeping her fingers hovered over me. "Ko, did you hear anything?"

"No baby, I didn't. Maybe he doesn't want to play." His words drop from his lips so innocently as her gaze levels on me. The asshole smirks and raises a brow. I'm half tempted to shave off the first chance I get.

"Please," I whimper as her light traces along the sides of my covered cock.

"I knew you'd always beg for me." Pandora winks. I help her pull my pants down to my knees and my boxers, letting my cock free. The cool air stinging me doesn't last long before my cock is engulfed by the heat of her mouth. Her tongue runs along the underside and she tries to put as much of me in her mouth as she can. Hollowing her cheeks, she comes back up and lets me go with a pop, salivate dripping front of the head of my cock to her lips.

"Just as good as I thought," she says before taking me in her mouth again. This time moving faster. Taking me in, then moving back out, I moan as she works her tongue and cheeks.

"Let me guide you, baby," Kohen murmurs, his hand still around her neck. Him moving her turns me on even more. I'm sweating as I watch them work me up. His hand strains around her neck, his fingertips almost touching as he pushes her forward and brings her back. "I know what he likes."

Fuck, he most definitely does. I throw my head back as he slows her down with a tinge as she reaches the head of my cock. Her hands soon find my tightening balls. My hips instinctively meet her mouth for each stroke and the pressure building is about to fucking combust.

I watch Kohen as takes his other hand and carcasses her shoulder. Moving his hand down to her waist and yanks her dress down so her boobs pop out.

"I told you I'd get to take this dress off," he says with a smirk.

"Shut the fuck up delivery boy," I spit out, barely able to talk with pandora's lips around me. Kohen's eyes stare into mine as he caresses her right boob as he kisses her neck. I hear her grunt on my cock and I nearly fucking cum.

My hands find their way in Pandora's hair, fucking up her bun, but my mind isn't worried about that and neither is hers. I do my best not to move her head. I didn't crave control. I needed another connection to her. Her hair is soft in my grip as she works me. I thrust my hips harder, faster, and that's when she leans back, letting me go.

"Holy fuck," I mutter as she stands in front of me. "Who's the tease now?"

"I want to see you with Ko. I need our love to come full circle. Can you do that?" She says breathlessly.

"Fuck yes," I say and any lingering worries I could have about adding a third to Ko and I's relationship wash away. Pandora was always meant to be a part of our circle. She's the hope that holds us together. That keeps me on my toes and brings us life. She's ours and it took me way too fucking long to see what Kohen did a year ago.

Kohen comes to stand. Before he can properly blink, my hands are on him, smashing my lips to his. Kohen's lips are one of my favorite places to be. He grips my throat and brings me impossibly closer as we fight for dominance in our kiss. I walk him back against a wall trying to win this battle, but we both know I have no problem losing. I'd lose to him and Pandora any day if it meant having them by my side.

His body presses into mine and I love the harsh ridges of his lean body. I let my hands roam over his body with his hands still around my neck, slightly tightening and loosening. He fucking loves choking. I chuckle between our kisses.

Pandora must be ready because her hands enter our party and are racing up my back and over me to Kohen, who lights up in our kiss as she joins us.

I break our kiss and trail my lips down the side of his neck, biting and nipping at him as my hands press against his heated skin. The slight coverage of sweat makes his dress shirt stick to his skin and I see Pandora's hands unbuttoning his shirt and sliding it off his arms.

"Think you can take me?" I say, turning Kohen around to face a smirking Pandora.

"You know I fucking can," Kohen says as he launches his lips toward Pandora. She meets his kiss, pressing her body up against his and I fucking fall in love with the sight.

I press my cock into Kohen's ass and he moans into Pandora's mouth. I reach to his front and unbuckle his pants and yank them down, boxers included. Kohen's cock is unleashed and pre-cum leaks from the head. Fuck, my tongue yearns to lick it off him, but I resist, taking my finger instead and swiping it up to press into the hole in his ass. He jerks away before leaning back into me.

"Line yourself up with Pandora," I say on a breath. Working his hole with my sweaty fingers, I watch as he moves with utmost concentration as he grabs Pandora and lifts her up to wrap her legs around his waist, her heels digging into me as she focuses on Kohen's lips on hers.

He lines himself up and she sinks down on him as I slide a finger in. A little pain and pleasure mixing in his face. I trust my finger, but he already groans for more as he pounds into Pandora, who meets him thrust for thrust, digging her heels in his ass.

I growl as I line myself up with his entrance. I exhale as I enter, kissing his back as I slide in, inch by inch, making sure he's okay. We are normally much more prepared when we are together, but this time it's just us in this damn closet in a museum in Paris. Even without all our shit, I wouldn't have this any other way. I only hope I'm not hurting him.

I thrust and hear both of them moan. My favorite fucking sound. I slide back, holding Kohen's hips as I plunge forward again. I hear him rasp as he is then moved into Pandora and I could stay here forever. Me and them, for life, in this damn closet.

"I love you, I love you both so fucking much," I say, thrusting again. They both groan, and Pandora opens her eyes to look at me. Her brown eyes peer into mine and her lips are slightly open as her chest rises with each breath she takes. I can feel Kohen tense as we await her response.

She smiles, throwing her head back, hitting the wall. "I love you, the both of you, so much it hurts my chest," she says.

"I love you," Kohen says, kissing her lips before turning towards me as much as he can. "And I love you."

I meet his lips and kiss him again. I thrust forward again and this time I cum. My cum shoots inside his ass and I can feel his cum leaving him as he jerks into Pandora. She lets out a long groan as her body goes slack.

"Fuck, that was hot," she mutters, her legs sliding down from Kohen's waist. I pull out of Kohen, using my fingers to push my cum back into him. It's pointless, but I fucking love the sight. The possession that fills my chest.

I reach down and grab Pandora's dress off the floor. The thing is heavy as shit, but I hold it ready for her to step back into it.

"What if I wanted to walk out there naked?"

"Step into the damn dress," I mutter, shaking the dress. She laughs, barely standing up straight as I pull her dress up her body and spin around to zip her back up. I hook the tiny metal at the top and she's trying to fix her hair I completely fucked up.

Kohen dresses and comes to stand in front of her, helping her with her hair and fixing her jewelry. It's such a perfect moment I keep my hands on the zipper of her dress as I don't want it to end.

Swallowing, I meet both their eyes as they stare back at me. I exhale, my nerves coming back. "We should be a family, like, share last names and all the shit," I say, trying to play it off like it's no big deal. But inside, my heart is fucking pounding. It is corny as fuck to say this after sex, yes, but I do it anyway. I can't. I won't let them go, even if they say no.

"We're already family," Kohen says with a small smile on his lips. "I vote for Harthwarn to be our last name."

"What? Melrose isn't cool? Melrose is cool as shit," Pandora argues. "Eros, break the tie." I watch them turn to face me again and I chuckle.

"Well, Harthwarn is the one that brought us together," I say, still hiding behind Pandora as we leave the closet.

"Okay, but I want a ring, one with two stones, one from each of you, and you need rings, too. I don't want bitches thinking you're single."

"A ring sounds perfect," Kohen says as he slides his hand into mine. I kiss his forehead as Pandora walks in front of us, describing the kind of ring she wants, changing her mind every thirty seconds.

"And one more thing." She says, stopping and turning around to face us. I raise my eyebrows and she only smiles. "Don't quit your job, Eros. At least not yet."

"What, we talked about this—" I say, but Kohen cuts me off with a shake of his head.

"You love this, you need this. Just because I'm retiring doesn't mean you have to, too."

"But I do. I can't only think about the Society anymore, I live for you two." I am confused why this isn't obvious to them. Working for the Society means giving your life away and I... I can't do that. I have them. I need to be here for them.

I wanna come home and see them, every day, for the rest of my life. I want to see Kohen in the kitchen and Pandora sitting on the counter. I want our Sunday painting sessions. I want them. I choose them.

"You'll be careful, you always were."

"That means I'd be paired with a new courier." I say, trying to convince them that this isn't a good idea.

"Who will never be as good as Ko, but will be essential to helping bring you home every day," Pandora says, grabbing my hands and bringing them to her lips.

"You love being a Guard, and you will continue to be a Guard," she says. I stand breathless for a moment. I... I've been moping about all day thinking this was my last, and they noticed. They noticed it and knew that this makes me happy.

They choose my happiness too.

I smile as Pandora turns back around, going on about what her ring needs to have and what our ceremony will be like.

"We did it," I whisper to Kohen. He smiles warmly, gazing at Pandora as we walk back towards the ballroom. We may have had to get our hands dirty, but we got what we both always wanted, a family. People to reply on, to fall back on. People to love and protect. We have people we can call ours. A place where we are wanted.

"Yeah, we sure did."

ENJOYED MY LITTLE DISASTERS?

Leave My Little Disasters a review at Amazon and Goodreads.

I would be so grateful if you left a review for this book. Leaving a book review is like buying the book a million times over and is a great way to support authors! One review could lead to more readers finding another book they love.

Your support is the lifeline for many authors. Reviews give us the chance to receive feedback on what readers, like you, are enjoying!

Thank you in advance for your support! A review left anywhere, like amazon, goodreads, storygraph, social media and beyond is incredibly helpful for authors and readers alike!!

Other Books in the Darkest Desires Series

Did you enjoy My Little Disasters? Then check out all these other amazing books in the Darkest Desires Series!
<u>See the whole series on Amazon.</u>
https://www.amazon.co.uk/dp/B0DGGMB42F

<u>Forgive Me Father</u> by Ryan Reeve
A serial killer priest and his tattoo artist companion team up with a lost soul to exact revenge.

-

<u>Perfect Poppy</u> by Casia Pickering
A therapist catches the eye of a mortician when she goes feral against toxic men.

-

<u>Little Crane</u> by Jorjor Battle
A poisoner and a professional assassin team up to take down a human trafficking ring in their town.

-

<u>Her Lips to God's Hands</u> by Aurora Light

A serial killer meets her obsessed fan, throwing her perfectly controlled life into disarray.

-

<u>My Little Disasters</u> Jorjor Battle
A painter, a guard, and a courier take on the mafia to protect the ones they love.

-

<u>The Sinners Gambit</u> By Annie Gray
A top surgeon is kidnapped by a lonely serial killer who is infatuated with her, uncovering shocking revelations

-

<u>Beyond Death</u> by Morgan Dale
A trafficking victim turned serial killer vows revenge on those who've wronged her.

-

<u>The Bludgeoner and His Little Monster</u> by Daffodil Rae
A former nightclub host recruits his boyfriend, a brutal assassin, and a black market meat dealer to exact revenge on the fiends of his past.

-

<u>Fatal Dates</u> by KD Michaels
A female serial killer who goes after men on dating apps who are cheating on their significant other.

-

<u>My Murderous Wife</u> by Abigail Hunter

A woman cuts out the hearts of men to gain memories of her husband, until a murder goes wrong, and the man who rescues her looks all too familiar.

ALSO BY JORJOR BATTLE

<u>Stained Series</u>

Stained Perception

Stained Fate

<u>Darkest Desires: Season 1</u>

Little Crane

My Little Disasters

About the Author

Jorjor Battle is a Michiganer pursuing her dreams of becoming a dark romance author. She'd prefer to fall in love in real life but, for the time being, accepts her unhealthy obsession with love in the forms of books, tv shows, and movies. A couch, a blanket, a gallon of hot tea, chips in a bowl, a tv remote, a pillow, her laptop, her phone, her dog, and a book is *all* she needs to have a good time ;)

Follow her on social media to hear about upcoming projects and all things about being a writer and book lover!
Instagram: @readingjorjor
TikTok: @readingjorjor
Pinterest: @readingjorjor

Read on for a Sneak Peak into Little Crane

Prologue

Diora

"*There's a light in children's eyes that you just don't have, dear.*" My mom's words ring in my ears as if I am hearing them for the first time. I am only six, but it didn't seem to matter to my mom. Six years was more than enough to develop the light, according to her.

If I ever had the light, it died this day. It died the moment my mom gave up on me. It died the day they separated my sister, Juliet, and me.

Now that I was six and Juliet was eleven, Mom and Dad said things had to change. Juliet is excited about getting her own room. It's a sign that she is now a big girl. Older. More mature. She didn't know the real reason we were being separated.

I did, though. They didn't want Juliet to be tainted. "*Juliet is the last good thing to come from my womb.*" Juliet had the light Mom was talking about. I didn't. I could wear all the light pastel colors I wanted. Brighten any room with lamps and lights and I would never have the same light that Juliet does.

My princess pink blanket crumbles under our weight. All the work I did to make the perfect bed is wasted as my mom comes into my room saying she wants to talk. Who has talks with a six-year-old?

I sit beside her, and even then, I see the recoil she tries to hide. My smile falls as she stares at me. Eying me like a prey watches a predator. When the bedroom door shuts, Mom can be her true authentic self. The disgust, the fear, can shine through her facial muscles, and the honesty I wish she'd kept hidden for longer soaks the air.

"Mommy?" I ask as she carefully lays a hand on my head. She sighs as tears fall down her face, one by one. I wish I could make the fat tears go away, but I know I am the cause of them.

"You love your sister, don't you?" she asks. Patting my hair. Getting harsher with each pat. She slowly rocks herself back and forth, as she normally does when it's just me and her. She cries when it's only me and her. She says mean things when it's only her and me.

If Mom hates me so much, why is she only her truest self around me?

"How could you? Do you even know what love is, honey?" she mutters.

"I do," I say. "I love Juliet."

"Then why don't you be normal for her? If not for me, then for her?"

"What's wrong, Mommy?" I ask, reaching for her hand. Her skin is always soft, smooth, a luxury she doesn't let me touch, and yet I try, anyway. She snaps her hand away from me.

"Don't touch me, Diora," she quietly barks. *"Don't spread your evil."*

I shake my head, confused, yet not confused at all. It's as if I need to hear her say it again and again. The constant reminder that I'm not good. I'm not light. I'm not Juliet.

"I'm not evil," I say, and my voice breaks. I know it's not true. That I'm not normal, but I thought, maybe, if Juliet loves me... If Juliet loves me, why can't Mommy?

"What do you call playing in a dead child's blood, Diora? *Evil, bad spirited.*"

I swallow my words, not wanting to argue with Mommy. I stare at my mommy. Meet her scared eyes.

It wasn't. I wasn't. I shake my head as Mom's tears roll faster down her face. I wasn't playing with blood. I wasn't playing.

My mind jumps back to yesterday. The smooth consistency of the red liquid spread around my classmate, Darcy, when she jumped off the school play set and hit the cement.

Blood is bad? I blink as my mind races with words I can't speak. Mom won't believe me. She never does.

Blood is messy. I was trying to clean her up. Once I got there, once I got to her, I tried to put it back. I wasn't playing with her blood. It was soft, smooth, in my hands, but I was trying to help. I swear I was.

Mommy wouldn't believe me. Neither would Daddy. Or the play guard. Or Darcy's parents, who screamed in my face at the school's front office.

I knew this.

And yet, I still tried to help Darcy. That's what Juliet would have done.

But that doesn't matter.

They've written me off.

They've given up.

I watch silently as my mom's tears stream down her face, and her silent sobs wrack her body as she pats my head. She wraps her frail arms around my body and pulls me in for the last hug I'll ever get from her.

Her shirt is soft and wet from her crying. But I... I like the warmth her body gives me. I want to wrap my arms around her like I would when Juliet hugs me, but I don't think Mom will like that.

"Oh, baby, my little baby Diora. You're a monster."

A monster?

"You have to stay away from Juliet. You mustn't taint her, Diora." Her words come out sharp as she grips my head. She rocks me back and forth with her. I don't know what to do. Mommy is sad. I didn't... I knew... I wanted to... I don't know.

"Monsters are bad?" I ask. Her grip starts to hurt. My skin pulls in her tight grasp and my eyes hurt. I close them. The strain behind them intensifies. It hurts. It actually hurts this time.

"Monsters are bad, Diora," she says.

"I can't be a monster. I love Juliet, and I love you, too, Mommy." I wanna fix this. Fix my mommy, fix me. I try to look at her, but she won't let me move my head. She sobs out loud this time, and her tears wet my hair.

"I'm so sorry. I'm so sorry," she cries, and that's when I sense the sharp kitchen knife at my wrist. She slices vertically up my forearm and it burns. It hurts. I can feel it.

"I can't love a monster, baby."

"Mom!" I hear Juliet's voice on the other side of my door as that same smooth, creamy blood runs down my arms and onto Mommy and my bed. She's loudly crying as Juliet pounds on my door. Juliet starts crying, as if she knew.

My dad's footsteps are loud as he storms in with tears down his own eyes. I've never seen Dad cry. He rips the knife from Mom and swallows *her* in a hug. Her. Mommy. Not me.

My arm grows numb, and my princess pink bedding gets ruined. Messy. Bloody.

I blink, a single time, and I feel Juliet's little arms wrap around me. Mommy tries to grab for her, but Juliet dodges her. My blood smears on her arms as she hugs me. I enjoy Juliet's hugs. Juliet's hugs are soft and warm. I rest my dry cheek on her shoulder as she sobs into me.

I can't be a monster. If I'm a monster, Mommy will take me away from Juliet. I have to be good.

For Juliet. I'd do anything for Juliet.

Chapter 1

Diora

I like the texture of dirt and plants under my nails as much as I like skin and blood. Watching the four officers from the corner of my eye, I lift the hot kettle from the hot pot on my workstation and pour boiling water into four antique tea cups.

The four officers sit in metal chairs, designed to look like old fashioned dining chairs, around my round, stained glass table. They are gagged and bound, with nothing on except their t-shirts and underwear.

They thought they were flirting with a meek girl in a bar full of rowdy drunken men.

They didn't know the meek girl in front of them had been working on their capture for six months now.

I've been picking each of them up from their favorite after work bars for four weeks now, one at a time, keeping them drugged in my greenhouse in the forest on Laker Street.

My white gloves are covered in dirt smears as I pick off a few flowers of foxglove. I crush the pendulous bell-shaped flower into tiny pieces. The pretty pinks and purples make me smile as I sweep the crushed flowers into small tea packets.

Foxglove is a beautiful plant that has many uses, both as a poison and a medicine. It's one of the most beautiful poisonous plants, subjectively, and therefore, it is my favorite to use.

My scar from... from sixteen years ago now, shows on the inside of my forearm as I prepare the tea. I drop a tea bag into each mug of boiling water, letting the water soak up the properties of the plant. I inhale, feeling the chemicals from the plant sting my nose. This dose of poison is deadly, even to those in optimal health.

These officers are in perfect health, according to their last required physicals. How convenient is that?

How convenient was letting the perpetrators of my sister's nightmare free?

Doesn't seem so convenient now, does it?

Hearing a grunt, I turn around with two saucers with teacups on them in my hands. The officers wake up, the chloroform wearing off. It's not my favorite weapon of choice, but in a pinch, speed and effectiveness must come first. I had to get four largely muscled male bodies from the shed behind my greenhouse to the scene of their final show: my first crime.

Their murder.

"Hi, gentlemen," I say, setting everyone's teacups in front of them, including one in front of me. They struggle against their restraints, but they're too weak to break them. I made sure.

"I figure you must be confused, angry, maybe even upset, huh?" I ask, swishing my tea with a tiny spoon. "So was she."

Their grunts and heaving sound gross. I grimace as I glance at the clock above my work station. Two a.m. Hmm, I guess starting the show now is fine.

"You must not remember our first meeting at the police station, since most of you approached me first, kind of... Well, that's not important. What's important is that you know why your wives and children are going to miss you," I say, taking a sip of my own foxglove-filled tea. I let my own tea soak longer, since I prepared it earlier than theirs, though I won't be drinking as much as they are. It's unfair to be bad without punishment.

Being bad cannot go without punishment, even if it is only in reaction.

Murder is wrong. No matter how much I'm itching to do so. No matter what reason I muster up to justify why I'm doing what I'm doing.

Sipping on my tea, my breathing changes as I consume the poison. Though, I know I'm not dying today. I've just started my vengeance for my sister, Juliet, and I will not die before I've got my greedy hands on the woman who orchestrated the worst night of Juliet's life.

Getting up, I ungag each man, letting their slobbered white rags pile in the mini black fireplace by my workbench. They cough and gurgle as they regain the power of speech.

I stumbled upon this greenhouse when I was a kid, and have been rooted in these four walls since. It's big enough to have a few rows of plants I've accumulated over time, with floor to ceiling arched windows. The intricate designs on the windows and ceilings give the little house an ethereal vibe.

Like an old haunted house, with crown molding and sculptures, this greenhouse has become my safe space. Even with all the windows, I'm not worried about being caught. This is the one space I can unleash my urges, and now I've found the perfect victims to satisfy my craving for death.

"You all are gross," I say, conscious of the contaminated heat mixing with their bodies' smells and germs that touch my skin. Cold nights remind me of my sister. How she loves cold nights. She loves bundling up in blankets by the fire watching TV. I love spending time with her, so I let her wrap me in her softest blankets, too.

Juliet is the only person on this earth who loves me, and *they* dared to hurt her.

I failed to protect her.

That won't happen again.

"What the hell are you doing?" the tallest man spits. His name is Josh Panko. He's been on Litchfort's police force for over twenty years. Has a wife and two kids, aged seven and eleven. His hobbies include watching football and going to the bar. Anything but spending time at home with his wife and kids.

"Don't you hurt my fucking wife, you fucking bitch." Now, Kyle is different. Kyle loves his wife, and he has no kids. His hobbies include sitting on his back porch with a beer and a book in his hands that he never reads.

Growls and yells never bothered me. They don't process in my brain like they do my sisters. She gets scared when people get mad. It's why I never get mad. Their anger would scare her into these men's submission. That's why I'm here and she isn't.

"I'm not going to hurt your wife or your children—not physically."

"Of course you're fucking not. Untie us and maybe we'll let you off easy. Kidnapping officers is a high offense," Josh Panko says, trying to bargain with me. I turn around to face the four men. They look a mix of pissed off and amused. As if something is funny.

Maybe this is funny to them. A girl like me kidnapped four men like them. I'm not necessarily strong, and they weigh about two-hundred pounds each, and yet, what they have yet to realize is that, even with all the odds against me, I still got them here, bound and gagged.

"I'm not hurting your wives or children because they are good. I'm killing you because you're evil."

"Won't killing us make you evil, too?" Josh asks, though, I've already thought this through.

"No, it won't," I say, taking my seat again and sipping my tea.

"How in the fuck would it not make you evil, too?" Kyle Montery asks, spitting as he's talking. Fear is clouding his thoughts. He's unable to keep a cool head in any situation, so it doesn't come as a surprise to see him slipping first. His anger is causing his chest to heave, his pulse decreasing with his increasing breaths.

The foxglove in the air is already working on him. It slows the pulse, and I see by the effort he exudes, he's working overtime to control his breathing.

"I can't become evil. I already am," I say. My single strand of pearls around my neck becomes hot and heavy as the room's temperature rises, aware of the next stage of my plan taking place. My windows begin to fog. I can't contain my smile.

"Be good, then. Let us go," Josh tries. He must think he's playing me. He's an annoying kind of blond—not golden enough to appear soft, but bright enough to make my eyes twitch. His blue eyes irk me, too; they're too blue. The kind of blue that appears right as lightning strikes, on the verge of being white.

I hate it.

I hate him.

"You want to leave before you know why you are here?" I ask, not making a single move to untie my guest. My own chair is made of the same metal, painted white to help create the tea party ambiance.

"We don't give a fuck," Kyle barks. His eyes move rapidly back and forth as the sweat drips down his forehead. I prefer Kyles over Joshes in this world. Kyle is true to human nature. No one is calm when their lives are threatened. He's showing me all his cards, and exactly how he feels, while Josh is hiding. He hides behind the facade of control.

"Okay," I say, shrugging my shoulders. I rise from my chair, my white t-shirt stained with plant stems and sweat clinging to my chest as I move to stand behind Kyle. His brown hair stinks, and he shakes violently, yelling incoherent curses. Still, I lace my fingers in his hair and lay my head over his greasy hair.

My cheek itches with the nastiness that is Kyle's greasy hair, but I persist.

"Hmm, well, the least you could do is let me give you a name," I say. I grin as my eyes meet my silent captive. Lewis Karplie. He hasn't uttered a word, and I think he may be the only person to recognize me.

He hadn't recognized me when they approached me in the bar, but I think he does now.

Lewis Karplie is the only Black officer here. As much as I wanted to give Lewis a pass, an excuse for a fellow Black person trying in this world, I can't.

He has three kids and a wife, who all strive to do their best in their own pursuits of life. He spends the most time with his family, game nights, movie nights, dinners, he makes those.

He's a seemingly good dad, like the rest of these officers, doing the bare minimum to have a family. But then, the lights go off, and we see the truth.

The shadows that reveal the darkest truths of every single person in this room, including me. We are not good. We are evil. We've done bad things, and now we must pay the price.

Lewis jumps back in his chair when his eyes meet mine. He is the one person I debated excluding from tonight's show. Lewis had hesitation that night. When my sister and I came to the police station to report her rape, he had the nerve to give us hope.

All that pity withered away the moment the politician's name left our lips and suddenly, Lewis Karplie's face turned to stone. He refused to help us any further and ripped the report to shreds.

"You know, Lewis. Why don't you share with the class?" I command as my grip gets tighter in Kyle's hair to keep him still. Kyle's calmed down now, still shaking like a leaf, realizing he can't break his restraints. He's getting weaker. They all are, whether they know it or not, as the poison works in their systems.

The steam from the tea has been filtering in their systems quickly, since I placed their cups directly under their noses.

Lewis begins to convulse, his locs shaking as he shakes his head no repeatedly. Wide brown eyes pierce into mine for a split second before Josh gets the man's attention.

"Lewis, what do you know? Lewis, say it. Now."

"I-I don't, I can't believe—" Lewis chokes.

"Lewis, if you don't tell your partners why they're here, I'll slit Kyle's throat right now," I say, letting Kyle's hair go with one hand and pulling the dagger from my belt holster. It was situated behind my back, like how they turned their backs to me, to Juliet.

"Lewis," Kyle hisses as the sharp end of my dagger traces the side of his neck.

"Okay, okay. God," Lewis pants as dread covers his skin. He shivers, and he meets my eyes again and mutters the name I wanted to hear. "Juliet Moss."

"Ahh, yes, Juliet Moss. You are right Lewis. Ring any bells, boys?" I say, moving away from Kyle and to Lewis. I stand behind him now, wondering if giving him mercy is worth the pain they helped cause that night.

A quick death for answering my question.

Or a slow death for turning my sister and me away?

"Juliet?" The fourth and final member of our party speaks. Orlando Jones. He had been quietly muttering to himself until the reason they are here was revealed.

Orlando Jones is the fourth member of this clique. These four are famous on Litchfort's force, for being Yara Holdings favorites. A.k.a. her minions, cleaning her dirty doings up.

Orlando doesn't have a wife or kids. He lives alone in his apartment on Monroe Street. He often sits in the dark; for what, I'm not quite sure. He always lets the TV play in the background, but I can tell he doesn't watch it.

Not that I cared that these could be completely innocent men who made a mistake. A mistake of brushing off the crying girls trying to report the most powerful politician in Michigan. A battle we won't want to fight, they'd say, as they turn us away.

Even then, they'd be sitting in this greenhouse filled to the brim with poison and my need for vengeance and repentance.

"My sister, of course, it could be hard to remember one of many victims who have tried to come forward against Yara

Holding's crimes, but..." I inform them, letting my sentence drop off as realization of what they did to end up here sparks to life in their minds.

Yara Holding is working her way up to a powerful seat in government—the senate majority leader. Currently working as a lawyer, she builds connections the quickest way she knows how: giving powerful, hungry, greedy men already in power what they want most: a night without consequences.

She has these men's jobs on the end of her whip. Instead of protecting people, the whole point of their jobs, they let Ms. Holdings' crimes be swept under the rug.

It's fine, though. Cause I'm here.

Deciding that Lewis Karplie will be dismissed from this party first, I release my hold on Kyle. Lewis shakes in his chair as I approach him. Bringing a tea cup up to his lips, I force a drink down his throat, jerking his chin upward, so the only way the drink can go is down, and he swallows the foxglove like a champ.

Despite the shaking and the burning and his body's instinct to gauge the drink back up, I seal his lips closed with my hand. Regardless of how much seeps through, I've got enough in his system for the effects to finish him.

The men shout, and Orlando Jones even cries at the sight. Even then, nothing has changed my desired outcome. Lewis Karplie's body begins to shut down. With my hand so close to his neck, I can feel his pulse slow tremendously, and his pupils become smaller as the foxglove takes down his body with each second that passes.

He stares right into my eyes as he dies. He doesn't say anything. Maybe he'd accepted his fate long before I walked over. Maybe he realizes you can't argue with evil when you're evil yourself. Maybe he knows, deep down somewhere, that he deserves this.

Life drains from his face, and he goes slack in my hands. Letting his head drop, I walk back to my seat, taking a deep breath before sipping my tea, letting the burn in as I stare at Lewis Karplie's dead body. I wonder if everyone's first kill is like this.

I gaze down at the light pink liquid in my cup, unable to hide my smile any longer. My black, frizzy hair covers the sides of my face as I stare down. A giggle slips past my lips, and that's what gets the men to quiet down.

I look up, meeting each of their eyes as fear drips into them. Understanding their situation now, pleads of mercy fill my little house. The sounds bounce off the arched windows, and despite how cold it is at this time of night, it's boiling in here.

I watch as the foxglove I've injected them all with prior to them waking up speeds its effects as their bodies fight harder. They'll die faster without me having to lift another finger.

"I'll fucking kill you," Josh whips at me, cracking his calm boy persona.

"You're already dead, Josh. All of you are," I inform as I stand to pick up each of their teacups and dump the liquid over the remaining three officers.

Those were more for set up. I didn't know who'd figure out why they were here first, so I placed a teacup in front of each of them. "I injected a lethal amount of foxglove into your systems about an hour before you all woke up. With the combination of your panic and the chemicals from that plant and many others, it's only moments before you drop dead, like Lewis."

Splashes of the now lukewarm tea hit my exposed feet and their faces as they spit and scream in surprise. Their anger has changed to pleading as the weakness in their bodies registers in their minds. Their pleads anger me further, proving why Lewis deserved the quick death I offered him.

"Hurting yourself too is an unusual style of dealing with guilt, my dear Diora, but I must say, I'm impressed with what I've seen," a slick, aged voice speaks. The sudden sound makes me jump from my seat, reaching for my dagger.

Who the hell is here?

I'm not the biggest fan of blood. Using knives and daggers isn't my specialty, either, but I've trained in using multiple weapons since the start of my vengeance mission.

"Help! Please help us!" Orlando shouts, drool spouting from his mouth. The woman grimaces before pulling out what appears to be a Ruger LCP Max, but to be honest, I'm not sure. I only know how to shoot a gun, and the one she has is small enough to fit in her white tweed purse.

I'm more concerned with why she's here. I glare at the unknown woman. Doesn't she see I'm in the middle of something?

"I'll shoot right between your eyes if you speak out of turn again, Orlando," she says, keeping the weapon trained on him. Her attention snaps back to me as she steps into the light. She's an older Black woman, maybe in her fifties or sixties, in what could be her Sunday best. Her tweed dress fits impeccably, and she slinks into the room with kitten heels on. Her hair is dyed brown, with a few grays peaking out, and her eyes are brown and sharp, setting me on edge.

I'm pissed she interrupted my night. It was going exactly how I planned, and here this woman comes. Now I have to kill her, too.

Rolling my eyes, I watch the new player on the scene.

I can't speak unless she speaks to me, that much I know. She has the gun, so she has the power at the moment.

I don't know if she's on their side, acting as their savior, and that is my biggest concern. It looks to me she knows them, yet threatening to kill one of them makes me unsure about why she's really here.

I can't have her messing this up. I spent six months planning tonight, and I will not let her ruin it.

Orlando's body shakes harshly before slumping over, his head hitting my delicate watercolor inspired tablecloth, death finally taking him. Now, all that's left are Josh and Kyle, who is still spitting out curses and thrashing in his chair nailed down to the floor.

Josh's eyes have gone dark, as the hope of besting me has died. I didn't think much more would make me happier but this realization from the man who turned my sister away from reporting her sexual assault and making her feel dumb because "how can a woman sexually assault another woman" is the perfect icing on my cake.

Juliet Moss deserves justice. She deserves the world, and I'll give that back to her.

"Two to go and you've barely touched these men, Diora. Darling, you're destined for great things," the woman says, coming to stand closer. She only takes a few steps, but her smile—it's her smile that has me flinching.

Friend or foe is the question blaring in my mind, and I can't make the determination. I stand this time and make a show of my weapon. My knife now comes in front of my chest, the blade facing away from me. It pisses me off that she's made me do this. Hold this knife.

The poison in the air isn't enough to take someone with as much energy as her.

"Who are you?" I ask. Her smile doesn't falter as she sees my weapon, and from the way my arms line with goosebumps, I get the sense that she's stronger than me. Way fucking stronger.

"I'm Mrs. Jay, soon, you'll be calling me Mother," she says, tilting her head with a sickly sweet smile. "What's the plan, darling? What's next in this lovely show you're orchestrating?"

"Why would I tell you?" I snip. I don't know this woman, and yet here she comes, guns blazing and asking me for answers.

She moves the gun toward me this time, and I huff before answering.

"Let the poison kill them," I say, not entirely sure why I'm offering such information to her. If she kills me, then she could let the rest of these pigs free, and I will not let that happen.

But if she's here to... watch, maybe I can finish out this plan before she kills me.

If she kills me. I sense that's not in her plans tonight. If it was, she'd have done it already.

"Mmm, that's why you've planted the plant in all their yards. Hmm, you plan to dump their bodies close by, make the deaths seem like an accident. A coincidence?"

How did she know that? She didn't need me to tell her anything. She must have been here the whole time.

"One Google search would tell anyone the plant was poisonous. Have you thought about that?"

"Why Google what you don't know?" I ask.

"Hmm, well, I can't interfere. That would be against the rules of Mortes Ostium, but I'm getting the feeling you won't have a problem with meeting their requirements," she says, standing by the table now. "Do you have an extra chair? I'd love to watch."

Who the hell is this woman, and what the hell is Mortes Ostium? The confusion makes my skin itch uncomfortably. My eyes dart between each living being in the room. Do I take the chance to trust this person, or do I kill her now? Could I kill her now?

"Darling, I've been in the game for thirty years; you're not beating me today. Now, please," she says, waving her hand to the lack of a chair behind her. I drag the stool from my workstation for myself and give her my height appropriate chair. She sits, smoothing out the skirt of her dress before clasping her hands under her chin and staring at me.

I've got the height advantage, but it doesn't feel like I have the advantage. She's completely at ease, even staring up at me.

"What the fuck is going on?" Kyle shouts, seeming not to operate on any other voice level other than loud. Maybe I should move this along and kill them quicker—no. I have to stick to my plan.

"I don't know," I mumble, keeping my eyes on the threat in the room.

"I figure now is best to talk, Diora Moss. I'd like you to join me."

"Join what?" I ask, scrunching my eyebrows. Is she talking about that Mortes group? What could this lady possibly want with me?

"My company, Haven Corporation, honey. I've been trying to spark creativity in my life, and I think you are the perfect fit," she says, booping my nose with one of her perfectly manicured nails, which causes me to flinch back and glare.

Does this woman have no fear? How has she gotten to such a state where she boops a person's nose who is in the middle of committing four murders?

"Perfect fit for what?"

"Killing people, of course. After thirty years, the act gets boring—dull even—until you find that spark again and I believe you to be my spark, Diora." The woman says as she digs in her large purse. "Here's a phone, once you've decided to join, give me a call, my contact is under Mother, and I'll give you future instruction," she says, sliding a compact flip phone on the table toward me.

I catch it, tossing it on my workstation. My brows furrow in confusion as I accept the phone, but I know there's not much I can do. She's killing people, I guess, but who? And why? Will I have time to complete my own mission if I link up with her? Do I have a choice?

"Haven is my personal company, but Mortes Ostium is a separate society for people like us. I have no say over whether you'll be admitted into that," she says. Her words still don't clear any confusion I have as the names get muddled in my head. "Collect a sample of each of their blood on microscopic blood slides for safekeeping, and don't forget I know that you're who killed these four men, and I know where you did it, so think wisely before deciding whether to call me or not."

Her face drops the lovely smile she had into a sharp glare. I watch as she remains seated at the table and Kyle and Josh attempt to blink away their blurred vision, which won't work.

The woman also sets blood slides on the table, carefully this time. As I take the four of them from her, my brows furrow.

"Go ahead, get a drop of blood from each dead person here." She smiles encouragingly and motions her hands toward Lewis's dead body.

Slowly rising from my chair, I take my knife and slice Lewis's arm, letting blood drop onto the slide before closing it up and setting it on my workbench.

My gaze flies between my captees and her as I collect their blood and place the slides on my bench.

"Let us fucking go, you bitch," Josh tries to demand. His voice comes out weak and shaky.

"No," I say, sipping on my cold tea as I watch the mysterious woman. "Not until you die."

I wait till Josh and Kyle's heads hit the table before I collect the blood from them. I have no idea what I'm going to do with these slides, but it seems better to do what the crazy lady says.

"How fun was this?" the woman says now that it's just her and me here. "Keep these, and someone will come to collect them and put them in your file with Mortes Ostium. Remember that, and I'll be expecting your call to work for me soon, darling."

She leaves with one final glance at the room filled with death.

Now it's just me, four bodies, and a mountain of confusion.

Little Crane

BLURB

Diora Moss is a crane in this house of dogs.
Elliot Jay is a puppet whose strings have snapped.

Diora Moss has only loved one person, her sister, and when a group of politicians hurt her sister, she can only think of one way to get justice. To kill everyone involved.
So when she does and gets caught by a monster much scarier than her, she's recruited to join an organization of hitmen, where she meets him.
Elliot Jay is a simple man with gray morals. As a top hitman in his family's organization, there is not much that bothers him except for one thing: kids. So when he finds out the organization's leader is involved with the disappearance of recruits, he gets the newbie Diora Moss to help save the kids.

A florist and a season serial killer find themselves entangled in more than work as they betray the people closest to them for revenge.

Little Crane is a full-length romance novel set within the Darkest Desire Anthology Series.

9 7 9 8 9 8 8 3 2 8 0 3 2